KAT THE TIME EXPLORER
by Emma Bradford

Ten-year-old Kat Thompson is excited about spending a year with her aunt, Jessie Adams. Kat's excitement turns to amazement when she discovers what Jessie is working on in her basement physics lab. Her aunt has found a half-finished time machine—along with notes about how to finish it.

With Kat's help, Jessie sets out to complete the device. But it's a lucky accident that enables Kat to start up the machine. The two are sent spinning back to London in 1851.

Kat and Jessie are thrilled to learn they've arrived at the time of the Great Exhibition. They can't wait to begin exploring the first world's fair.

All too soon, however, the adventure becomes a wild search. For Kat and Jessie discover that their traveling bag—with the time machine—is missing. Without it, they are stuck forever in the past!

STARDUST CLASSICS SERIES

KAT

Kat the Time Explorer

Stranded in Victorian England, Kat tries to locate the inventor who can restore her time machine and send her home.

Kat and the Emperor's Gift

In the court of Kublai Khan, Kat comes to the aid of a Mongolian princess who's facing a fearful future.

Kat and the Secrets of the Nile

At an archaeological dig in Egypt of 1892, Kat uncovers a plot to steal historical treasures—and blame an innocent man.

LAUREL

Laurel the Woodfairy

Laurel sets off into the gloomy Great Forest to track a new friend—who may have stolen the woodfairies' most precious possession.

Laurel and the Lost Treasure

In the dangerous Deeps, Laurel and her friends join a secretive dwarf in a hunt for treasure.

Laurel Rescues the Pixies

Laurel tries to save her pixie friends from a forest fire that could destroy their entire village.

ALISSA

Alissa, Princess of Arcadia

A strange old wizard helps Alissa solve a mysterious riddle and save her kingdom.

Alissa and the Castle Ghost

The princess hunts a ghost as she tries to right a long-ago injustice.

Alissa and the Dungeons of Grimrock

Alissa must free her wizard friend, Balin, when he's held prisoner by an evil sorcerer.

Design and Art Direction by Vernon Thornblad

This book may be purchased in bulk at discounted rates for sales promotions, premiums, fundraising, or educational purposes. For more information, write the Special Sales Department at the address below or call 1-888-809-0608.

Just Pretend, Inc.
Attn: Special Sales Department
One Sundial Avenue, Suite 201
Manchester, NH 03103

Visit us online at www.justpretend.com

Kat
the Time Explorer

by Emma Bradford

Illustrations by Kazuhiko Sano
Spot Illustrations by Tim Langenderfer

Stardust
CLASSICS

Just Pretend, Inc.
Attn: Publishing Division
One Sundial Avenue, Suite 201
Manchester, NH 03103

Stardust Classics is a registered trademark
of Just Pretend, Inc.

First Edition
Printed in Hong Kong
04 03 02 01 00 99   10 9 8 7 6 5 4 3 2

Publisher's Cataloging-in-Publication
(*Provided by Quality Books, Inc.*)
Bradford, Emma.
    Kat the time explorer / by Emma Bradford; illustrations by
Kazuhiko Sano; spot illustrations by Tim Langenderfer. -- 1st ed.
    p. cm. -- (Stardust classics. Kat; #1)
    SUMMARY: Kat and Aunt Jessie time travel to nineteenth-century
London, and are thrilled to learn they've arrived just in time to visit
the Great Exhibition.
    Preassigned LCCN: 98-65896
    ISBN: 1-889514-11-X (hardcover)
    ISBN: 1-889514-12-8 (pbk.)

    1. Time travel--Juvenile fiction. 2. Great Exhibition--(1851:--
London, England)--Juvenile fiction. 3. London (England)--Juvenile
fiction.
    I. Sano, Kazuhiko, 1952- II. Langenderfer, Tim. III. Title.
    IV. Series.
    PZ7.B7228Ka 1998   [Fic]
                                    QBI98-683

Contents

CHAPTER ONE

Time on Her Hands

Kat gave her watch a shake. Surely it wasn't working! It seemed like she'd been lying there for hours, staring at the ceiling. But only a few minutes had passed.

It's going to be a long year, Kat thought. She stretched out, almost knocking her Irish setter off the bed.

"Sorry, Newton," said Kat. She patted the dog's silky coat as she looked around the room. Her room—at least for the next year.

Sighing, Kat rolled off the bed. She walked over to an old globe that stood on a wooden stand. Slowly she turned it, tracing a line from her home in Winchester to South America.

South America—that's where Kat's parents were. Both her mother and father were college teachers. This year, however, they wouldn't be in the classroom. Instead, they'd be studying the plants of the Amazon rain forest.

Kat shook her head. "Maybe I should have gone with Mom and Dad after all," she said to Newton.

While her parents were away, Kat was living with her mother's younger sister. Moving in with Aunt Jessie had seemed like a great idea at first.

For one thing, Jessie lived just across town. That meant Kat wouldn't have to leave her friends or school. Ten-year-old Kat had lots of plans for this year. In just a month, she'd be going to middle school for the first time.

Kat had thought that staying with Jessie would be fun too. Her aunt was a scientist, like almost everyone else in Kat's family. She was a physics researcher at the same college where Kat's parents taught. Jessie knew about strange, amazing things like quarks and quasars.

But Kat hadn't seen much of her aunt lately. Jessie spent most of her free time in her basement lab. She was working on something important, she'd said. Kat was curious, but she didn't want to bother Jessie. So she'd been trying to stay out of the way.

Now Kat sighed and turned to Newton. "I can't wait for school to start," she said. "That will keep me busy."

Suddenly Newton lifted his head. He listened for a moment, then barked.

"What's up?" Kat asked the big dog. As if in answer to her question, the doorbell rang.

"Oh, it's just someone at the door," said Kat. "Jessie will get it."

But a few seconds later, the bell rang again.

Newton jumped off the bed and scratched at the bedroom door. "Okay, okay," said Kat. "Take it easy. I'll go see who it is."

Downstairs, there was still no sign of Jessie. So Kat answered the door herself. She found an impatient-looking woman standing there, ready to ring the bell again.

"Delivery for Jessie Adams," the woman announced. She held a box out to Kat.

Kat signed for the package, then brought it inside. The box was small, square—and heavy. The return address read "Tempus Fugit: The Time Company."

Kat studied the RUSH label planted on top of the box. "I'd better get this to Jessie right away."

With Newton at her heels, Kat headed down the stairs.

Jessie's lab was at the back of the basement. As Kat neared the room, she saw that the door was partly open. She stuck her head inside. "Jessie!" she called.

There was no answer. Slowly Kat entered the lab, looking around curiously. There was no sign of Jessie—or of the "important" project she was working on.

"Well, I'll just leave this here," Kat said. She placed the package where Jessie would see it.

As Kat started back to the door, something caught her eye. A yellowed notebook lay open on the corner of the table. It was crammed with notes and weird drawings.

That was too much for Kat. She loved reading. Cereal boxes, ads on the sides of buses, people's T-shirts—it didn't matter what it was. If there were words, Kat had to know what they said. So she certainly couldn't leave without looking at the notebook. She climbed onto a stool and started to read.

In a minute, she forgot everything. Her parents, her aunt, and school. All Kat could think about were the words she was reading. She didn't even notice when Jessie entered the lab.

"Kat!" gasped Jessie as she put down an armload of books. "I didn't know you were here!"

Kat looked up. She jumped off the stool and threw her arms around Jessie.

"Jessie, this is fantastic!" she cried. "Where did the notebook come from? Are you really making a time machine? Will it actually work? Can I help you?"

For a moment, Jessie just stared at her niece. Then she threw up her hands and laughed. "I can see you've discovered

3

what I've been up to. And that you're as curious as ever." With a grin, she added, "Anyway, I'm stuck. It might help me to talk to you about it."

As Kat sat back down, Jessie pulled up another stool. "To answer your first question, I found the notebook in the study."

"I knew it!" cried Kat. "It's Great-uncle Malcolm's, right?"

Malcolm Adams had lived in the house for his entire adult life. Just last year, he'd died at the age of 93. Malcolm had left the house and almost everything in it to Jessie.

One of Malcolm's many interests had been science—especially inventing. He hadn't made much money or become famous from his inventions. But everyone in town knew about his sometimes wacky, sometimes wonderful ideas.

Jessie nodded. "Yes, the notebook is his. One day I found it tucked behind some books," she explained. "As soon as I started reading, I was hooked. Traveling through time—that's something every physicist wonders about!"

"So you're using his notes to build a time machine?" said Kat.

Jessie shook her head. "Not quite. His notes aren't complete. At first I didn't think the idea was anything more than one of Malcolm's wild dreams."

Jessie grinned again. "But then I found *this* in a corner of the basement." She reached under the worktable and pulled out a canvas bag. Unzipping the bag, she lifted something out.

"Jessie!" Kat gasped. "It's the time machine!"

CHAPTER TWO

A Treasure Hunt

Kat moved closer to study the machine. The device had the same boxy design as in Malcolm's sketch. Four knobs rose from the top, a different symbol above each. There were several buttons and a display panel. In the center of the machine was a square hole, and handles stuck out from two sides.

Now Jessie reached underneath the device. She snapped open a latch and unfolded four metal legs. When she stood the machine upright, it reached to Kat's waist.

Kat couldn't contain herself. "Does it work? Did Malcolm ever travel through time?"

"He certainly never went anywhere with this machine," replied Jessie. "He didn't finish it. So I've been using his notes to do just that. If I ever get done…Well, then I'll see if it really works."

"How far have you gotten?" asked Kat.

"Pretty far," replied Jessie. "But like I said, I'm stuck now. Besides, I'm waiting for a part I ordered."

"I almost forgot," said Kat, reaching for the package. "This arrived today. Is it what you're waiting for?"

"At last!" Jessie exclaimed, tearing off the wrapping. "It's the chronometer!" She lifted the shiny time-keeping device out of the box. "Perfect," she said softly.

Kat glanced at the notebook again. "The chronometer must go there," she said, pointing to the square hole.

"So I guess I've got myself an assistant," Jessie teased. Then she handed the chronometer to her niece.

Kat carefully lowered the timepiece into place. "Is the machine ready to go now?"

"Slow down, Kat," said Jessie. She pointed to the notebook. "Look at the drawing. What's missing?"

Kat studied the sketch for a few moments. Finally she shook her head. "I give up. What?"

"There doesn't seem to be a power source," said Jessie. "Not one that's familiar to me, anyway."

Kat thumbed through the notebook again. Jessie was right. There was nothing about electricity or batteries—or any other kind of power.

As she closed the notebook, something caught Kat's eye. "What's this?" she asked. She pointed to a sketch on the back cover. It was a drawing of a round medallion on a chain. Strange markings covered the surface of the medallion.

"I don't know," admitted Jessie. "I've studied that sketch again and again. But I can't see what it has to do with the time machine. And the notebook does include drawings of other inventions."

Jessie shrugged. "Anyway, you can see for yourself. This was in Malcolm's bag too." She opened a drawer and handed a silvery medallion to Kat. It was exactly like the one shown in the notebook.

"It's so light!" exclaimed Kat, dangling the medallion from its chain. "What kind of metal is this?"

"Titanium," said Jessie. "Just like the body of the machine. The metal is so strong and light that it's used in spacecrafts."

6

Kat turned the medallion over. There were symbols on the back too. "I wonder what it's for?" she said, handing the medallion to Jessie. "Was there anything else in the bag?"

"No great scientific secrets," replied Jessie. "Just a book—an encyclopedia of history. I guess Malcolm thought a history book might be useful if he traveled through time."

Jessie put the medallion away. "Well, since you're now my official helper, let's get to work. Maybe together we can figure out how this thing works."

~~

In a few days, Kat and Jessie had finished the time machine. At least it looked finished.

Jessie stood back. "I still don't know how it's supposed to be powered. But let's try it anyway."

"Great!" Kat exclaimed. "What can I do?"

Jessie frowned. "You can move out of the room. Just in case."

When Kat started to protest, Jessie held up a hand. "I'm responsible for you while your parents are gone. How could I ever explain if I made you disappear in a puff of smoke?"

Kat laughed at the thought. "Can I watch from here?" she asked as she moved to the doorway.

Jessie nodded. Then she began twisting knobs and pushing buttons. But no matter what she did, the machine just sat there.

Still, Jessie and Kat didn't give up. They discussed ways that the device might be powered. They even checked Jessie's work several times.

Finally Jessie decided there was nothing left to try. It was time to get to work on other projects. But she was happy to let Kat stay around to act as her assistant.

One morning several days later, Kat entered the lab. She found Jessie already hard at work. A stack of books sat on the table in front of her. "Are those for your next project?" Kat asked.

Jessie nodded, "Yes. I'm catching up on my reading. But I can't find one book I need: *The End of Time and Space.*"

"Do you want me to look?" asked Kat. "I think I saw it around somewhere."

"That would be a big help," said Jessie. "And take Newton along. He seems bored."

"Come on, fella," called Kat. "We're going to explore."

Kat knew that her search might take a while. Except for the lab, things in the house were as jumbled as Malcolm had left them. That didn't bother Jessie—or Kat. They were fond of Malcolm's collections and inventions. But the clutter did make it harder to find things.

Kat hurried through the old-fashioned kitchen and started her hunt in the dark-paneled library. She looked through shelves filled with books, old toys, rocks, shells, and model ships. The book wasn't there.

From the library, Kat moved on to the dining room. There she rooted through cabinets filled with mismatched dishes and silverware. Still no luck.

Her next stop was upstairs, in Malcolm's old bedroom. Jessie had turned it into a guest room.

Kat skimmed the shelves before moving to the window seat. Another pile of books sat on the cushion. And at the top of the pile was the book Jessie wanted.

Kat grabbed the book, then turned to go. But she moved

so quickly that Newton couldn't get out of the way.

To keep from tripping, Kat reached out to steady herself. And in so doing, she accidentally knocked the books off the window seat.

"Really, Newton," Kat said as she began to pick up the mess. "Sometimes I think you're glued to me."

Then she paused. One book lay open in front of her. But it wasn't a book at all! Between the covers was a hollow space. And nested inside was something familiar.

"A medallion on a chain," she said slowly. "Just like the one Jessie found. Except that this one is gold."

Kat hurried down to the basement. "Jessie!" she called. "Look what I found hidden in a fake book!" She held up the medallion.

Jessie's eyes widened in surprise. "Let me see that," she said. Opening a drawer, she removed the first medallion. Then she placed the two medallions side by side on her worktable.

"They seem to be exactly the same," she commented. "Except for the metals used." She shook her head. "I can't see that this helps us much. We still don't know whether the medallions have anything to do with the time machine."

"They must be important," insisted Kat. "Is it okay with you if I fool around with them?"

"I guess so," said Jessie slowly. "The machine isn't going to go anywhere without a power source. But don't touch it unless I'm here with you."

So while Jessie worked, Kat went through Malcolm's notes again. Then she moved to the corner where the time machine stood. She twisted knobs and pushed buttons. The machine remained coldly still.

Kat sighed. There had to be some secret to the machine.

Slowly and carefully, Kat ran her hands over the surface of the device. Inch by inch, her fingers pressed and prodded. She worked her way along the top, then to the sides.

Kat was pressing on the left side of the machine when it happened. There was a tiny movement beneath her fingers.

"This feels different," she muttered. She pressed the spot again.

"Jessie!" Kat cried. "I've found something!"

Jessie hurried over. While her aunt watched, Kat slid open a small, thin drawer.

"It's a secret compartment," said Kat. "You have to know just where to push!"

"What can it be for?" asked Jessie excitedly. "There's nothing in there."

"But look at the bottom of the drawer," said Kat. "See those hollow round spaces? I bet the medallions fit there!"

Quickly Jessie got the two medallions. Kat watched as her aunt popped them into place, chains and all.

Nothing happened. Then Jessie slid the drawer back into the machine. Nothing.

"Well, they fit," said Jessie. "But they don't seem to do anything."

"I was hoping that they might be the power source for the machine," said Kat.

"It doesn't look like it," commented Jessie. "Still, let me check the notebook one more time. Perhaps I missed some clue about what they're for."

While Jessie paged through the notebook, Kat experimented with the medallions. "Maybe they have to go in another way," she whispered to herself. "After all, there are lots of combinations you can make."

First she put the silver one where the gold one had been. Then she flipped them over. Nothing happened.

Kat kept trying until there was only one possibility left. "This is the last chance," she told Newton. She placed the silver medallion on the right—with the front showing. She set the gold medallion on the left—with the back showing.

Suddenly a strange humming sound filled the room!

"What's going on?" called Jessie. She jumped to her feet and started across the room. Grabbing the other end of the machine, she shouted, "Let go, Kat!"

But before Kat could move, a ray of sunlight shone through the small basement window. The light poured over the time machine and lit up the open drawer. At once the medallions started to glow. Swirling ribbons of mist rose up around Kat and Jessie.

In a matter of seconds, the basement lab faded from sight.

CHAPTER THREE

Lost in the Crowd

cocoon of mist completely surrounded Kat. She couldn't see or hear Jessie. And her stomach felt strange. It was as if she were in an elevator that had suddenly dropped 20 stories.

At last she felt solid ground beneath her feet again. The mist still blocked her vision. But now she could hear a steady sound: thump-thump-thump.

Suddenly a whistle screamed, and the ground began to shake. Kat looked about blindly, trying to make sense of it all. Where was she? And where was Jessie?

Just as she was about to shout Jessie's name, the mist parted. To her relief, Kat saw her aunt standing across from her. But nothing else was familiar. The basement lab had vanished. Now they stood in the corner of a huge, domed building. People were rushing in every direction. And beside Kat and Jessie was a wall of gleaming black iron.

"It's a train!" cried Jessie. "An old-fashioned steam loco-motive!"

As they watched, the train slowly inched forward. It came to a stop farther down the platform, hissing and spitting like a great dragon.

"What happened?" gasped Kat.

"It worked, Kat!" Jessie answered. "I don't know how,

but it did!"

"We've really gone back into the past," said Kat in a whisper. "Where do you think we ended up?" she asked.

"And when?" added Jessie. "I already checked the chronometer, and it says no time has passed. But from the looks of our clothing, we've gone back at least 100 years."

Of course! Until this moment, Kat had been too stunned to realize why her aunt looked so strange. At home, in their own time, Jessie had been dressed in her usual jeans and T-shirt. Now she wore a lovely floor-length dress. Her hair peeked out from under a broad-brimmed bonnet.

Kat glanced down. Her own clothing had changed as well. She was wearing a long dress too, though hers was simpler than Jessie's.

"How—"

Jessie interrupted. "I can't answer any questions yet, Kat." She glanced uneasily at the crowds. "We're in the shadows here, so I don't think anyone saw us arrive. But we'd better get the machine out of sight before we're noticed."

Jessie folded the legs of the device. "I'll put it in here," she commented, reaching for a black leather bag that stood at her feet. She opened the bag—and froze.

"What is it?" asked Kat. "Is something wrong?"

Her aunt pulled something from the bag. "Malcolm's book," she said in wonder. "Kat, this bag must be the canvas one we had the encyclopedia in."

"I can't believe it!" breathed Kat. "It changed to fit the time, just like our clothing. See," she added, pointing toward a man in the distance. "He has a bag just like yours."

Then she glanced at the drawstring purse that dangled from her wrist. "Let's see what's in here."

She opened the purse and began pulling out objects. "Nothing familiar," she said. "A silver-handled brush, a handkerchief, and some strange-looking bills and coins."

Kat dropped the items back into the purse and thought for a moment. "Wait a minute," she muttered. She began to pat the sides of her skirt.

"Kat, what are you doing?" asked Jessie.

"I'm checking to see if this skirt has pockets. I was just thinking about what I put in my pockets this morning. And Jessie, this is really weird," she added. "I had a folding hairbrush, a tissue, and some money."

"So the things that you had in your pockets ended up in the purse. Only they changed like our clothing did," said Jessie in wonder.

She eased the time machine into the leather bag. "Let's find a more private spot," she suggested. "I don't want any witnesses when we set the machine up to go back."

"Go back!" Kat echoed. "What are you talking about?"

"Listen, Kat, we don't how we got here. Or how the machine works. We only know that it *does* work somehow. I want to get back to the lab and start experimenting."

"But isn't being here the best experiment we can possibly make?" protested Kat. "What's the point of traveling back in time if we turn right around and go home?"

Jessie shook her head. "If we've really gone back in time, it could be dangerous. We could run into trouble. Or change history somehow."

"Not if we're careful. Please, Jessie. Let's at least find out where and when we've traveled to. Besides, we can always go back if we do run into trouble. And it's not like anybody will miss us at home."

"What about Newton?" asked Jessie. "We can't leave him alone."

"We don't need to worry about Newton," Kat replied with a grin. "As soon as he gets hungry, he'll head out the doggy door. He knows that Mrs. Chang next door will feed him."

Jessie glanced around the busy station. At last she came to a decision. "All right," she said. "We'll look around the train station. But we have to be careful about what we do or say. And we have to stay together."

"Okay," said Kat. "Now let's explore!"

"Just a minute," warned Jessie as she opened the bag. "I'm going to take the medallions out. It's obvious that they power this thing. And we don't want it to go anywhere without us."

She handed the gold medallion to Kat. "Here. You keep this one, and I'll hang on to the other."

Jessie slipped the chain over her head and tucked the medallion under her collar. Kat did the same.

"Now can we go?" begged Kat.

"Lead the way," laughed Jessie.

They headed for the middle of the station. The farther they went, the more crowded and noisy it grew. Passengers were boarding some trains and getting off others. Conductors shouted, and whistles blew.

As Kat and Jessie neared the trains, two men walked by.

"Do we buy our tickets at the exhibition?" one asked the other.

"I don't know," the second man replied. "I tried asking the conductor, but he didn't know German. And I don't speak English."

Kat's eyes lit up with excitement. "Jessie! Did you hear what they just said?"

17

"Yes," said Jessie. "Though I'm sure I misunderstood. He said he didn't speak English. But I knew what he was saying. And I don't understand more than a few words of German. At least I never did before."

"This must be one more thing the machine does for us!" exclaimed Kat. "Listen!"

They stopped and let the crowd mill around them. Kat realized that most of the people she heard were speaking English. But she also caught traces of conversations in several other languages. And she could understand every word!

"Amazing!" Jessie said in an excited whisper.

At that moment, a poster caught Kat's eye. "Jessie! Look!" she pointed. "That's the exhibition everybody's talking about."

Kat read the poster aloud: "'The Exhibition of the Works of Industry of All Nations, 1851.' Well, now we know what year it is."

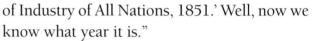

"And where we are," added Jessie. "I know a little bit about this. Malcolm showed me a book about the Great Exhibition. It was a huge world's fair that was held in London. There were things on display from all around the globe."

Kat noted the curiosity on her aunt's face. She decided to take advantage of it. "Jessie, can we go to the exhibition?" she asked. "Please?"

This time Jessie showed no hesitation. "Absolutely!" she declared. "We can't miss this." Then she seemed to remember her earlier worries. She added, "But we'll only be here for a while, Kat. I still want to get back home and learn more about how the machine works."

"I know," Kat said. "We don't have to stay for long."

Suddenly a thought struck her. "Do you mind checking Malcolm's encyclopedia? I'd like to know if there's anything in it about the exhibition."

"Okay," agreed Jessie. "As long as no one gets a close look at the book." She pulled the encyclopedia out, then dropped the bag at her feet.

While her aunt read, Kat stood and blocked the view of passersby. But she soon decided that Jessie had no reason to worry. People were caught up in their own business. A woman holding a small child by the hand rushed past. Her worried eyes darted about in search of someone. Then came an elderly couple, their heads buried in a train schedule. The old man carried a traveling bag just like Jessie's. So did the tall, balding man who stood next to Kat. He placed the bag on the floor and checked his watch. Then he frowned and gazed out over the crowd.

Kat was about to turn back to Jessie when a band of people approached. In the lead marched a large man, waving his hands wildly. "This way! This way!" he cried to his chattering followers.

Kat stepped aside to avoid being trampled. The group hardly seemed to notice her presence as it made its noisy way across the floor.

"Do you suppose they're all headed to the exhibition?" asked Kat.

When her aunt didn't answer, Kat turned to repeat her question.

Jessie was nowhere in sight!

19

CHAPTER FOUR

Tight Quarters

J essie! Where are you?" Kat cried. She whirled around, trying to spot Jessie in the crowd. But her aunt had disappeared.

Next to her, the tall man was searching for someone too. At least he can see over everyone's heads, thought Kat. Maybe I should ask him to look for Jessie.

Before she could speak, another wave of people came between Kat and the stranger. Just in time, she reached down and grabbed the leather traveling bag. For a few minutes, she was swept along with the crowd.

Kat fought her way back to the spot where she'd been standing. She remembered what she'd learned at camp: If you get lost, stay put. Surely Jessie would come looking for her.

Kat stood on her tiptoes. But she couldn't see Jessie anywhere.

Finally Kat sank back down on flat feet, fighting a feeling of panic. She tried not to think about being lost in a strange country—and a strange time. What if she and Jessie couldn't find one another?

To Kat, it seemed like she stood in one spot for hours. People continued to hurry past, paying her no attention. Her eyes swept the crowd, searching for Jessie's familiar face. But the only face she recognized was a worried one. It was the tall,

21

balding man. Bag in hand, he was hurrying toward the door.

"Kat! Thank goodness!"

Kat spun about to find Jessie behind her.

"Jessie!" she gasped in relief. "You gave me such a scare!"

"I gave *you* a scare!" exclaimed Jessie. "I had no idea where you were! One minute you were next to me. The next you were gone! I've been looking for you for more than ten minutes."

"It seemed a lot longer than that," admitted Kat. "Maybe we should get out of here," she suggested. "It might not be so crowded outside."

"Good idea," said Jessie. "Besides, we have to find a place to stay tonight. There must be some hotels nearby. Let's hope that the money in your purse will be enough to pay for a room."

Kat tucked the encyclopedia into her purse and they were off. They followed a steady stream of people out of the station. Once outside, they stopped in amazement. The street was packed with horse-drawn carts and carriages heading in all directions. People on foot hurried along the sidewalks and across the street. In fact, it was almost as crowded outside as it had been inside.

"Which way should we go?" asked Kat.

"Let's ask that policeman," suggested Jessie.

They made their way to a policeman who was standing on the corner. His response was hardly cheering.

"There are several hotels just down the street, ladies," he told them. "However, I'm not sure you'll find a room. The exhibition just started, you know. Seems like the whole world has turned up for it."

After thanking him, Kat and Jessie headed off in the direction he'd indicated.

"I can't believe this," complained Kat. "Will we have to go home just because we can't find a place to stay?"

"Don't give up yet," Jessie said with a smile. "Maybe we'll get lucky. And here's a hotel, so we'll soon know."

They headed for a granite building decorated with columns and carvings. Inside, gaslights cast flickering shadows over a large, high-ceilinged lobby. The carpet was thick, and oversized furniture lined every inch of the walls.

"It doesn't look crowded. At least not with people," Kat whispered. Speaking in a normal tone somehow seemed out of place here.

Still, there were no rooms to be had, the desk clerk informed them. "You might try the Royal Arms just down the street," he said. He sniffed and added, "It's not quite the finest establishment. So there may be a room available."

As they made their way back outside, Kat noticed that Jessie was breathing strangely. "What's wrong?" she asked with concern. "You're not sick, are you?"

"No," muttered Jessie. "It's these clothes."

When Kat looked blank, Jessie explained. "I can hardly take a deep breath. When my clothes changed, I ended up wearing a corset."

"A corset!" laughed Kat. She'd seen pictures of this strange undergarment. "No wonder your waist looks so tiny!"

"Just be glad nineteenth-century girls your age don't have to wear them," said Jessie. "Or you wouldn't be laughing. You wouldn't be able to."

"Well, let's find a room. Then you can take it off," said Kat. "Or loosen it a bit."

The Royal Arms proved to be a much smaller hotel than the first. There was no doorman, no thick rug—and no empty room.

"None at all?" Jessie asked the clerk, a young man with a pinched face and narrow shoulders.

"Not a one, miss," repeated the clerk. "I'm sorry to tell you that, seeing as how you've come such a long way. From America, are you?"

As Jessie and Kat nodded, the young man continued. "It's the exhibition, you know. I don't think there's a room to be had in all of London. Except perhaps at a lodging house. Though there aren't many of those suited to ladies like yourselves."

Jessie sighed deeply—then clutched her side. The corset was obviously bothering her.

"Could my aunt rest for a moment?" asked Kat. "Then maybe you could tell us where to find a lodging house."

"Of course," said the clerk, waving them toward a couch near the desk.

As Kat and Jessie sank down, a set of double doors across the room opened. Three middle-aged women came into the lobby. They stopped near Kat and Jessie. There they made their lengthy farewells, complete with promises to meet again for tea.

Two of the women left the hotel, but the third headed for the front desk. "Good afternoon, James," she greeted him. "My umbrella, if you please."

"Of course, Mrs. Dawson," said the clerk, reaching under the desk. He handed over a large black umbrella. "I trust your tea was enjoyable?"

"Very nice, as always," replied Mrs. Dawson. Umbrella in hand, she turned to go. But when the young man gave a rattling cough, she paused.

"James!" she said sternly, rapping the umbrella on the counter. "Did you take the advice I gave you last week?"

The young man's pale cheeks reddened. "Yes, ma'am," he muttered. "I did."

"I certainly hope so," said Mrs. Dawson. "One mustn't ignore one's chest, you know. There is nothing quite like a good mustard plaster."

"So you've said, ma'am," agreed James.

"Well, I think you should try a second treatment, James. Tonight."

"I shall do so," promised James. "Thank you once again for your concern."

He watched as Mrs. Dawson headed for the door. Kat noted that the clerk's expression was a mixture of fondness and relief.

Then the young man's eyes caught Kat's. He suddenly seemed to remember why she and Jessie were there. To Kat's surprise, his glance went from them back to Mrs. Dawson.

"Excuse me, Mrs. Dawson," called James, hurrying around the desk. "May I have a word with you?"

Mrs. Dawson stopped and gave him a questioning look. "Why, of course. Have you forgotten how to prepare a mustard plaster?"

"No," said James quickly. "It's not that." Taking her aside, he began speaking in a low voice.

As James spoke, Mrs. Dawson's head swung toward Kat and Jessie. She studied them with a look of interest.

"Very well," the woman said in a louder voice. "You are quite right to speak to me, James. One must be ready to offer a helping hand to visitors."

James led the woman toward Kat and Jessie. With a slight bow, he said, "Ladies, I would like you to meet Mrs. Dawson. She may be able to solve your problem."

"Mrs. Amelia Dawson," said the woman, holding out her hand to Jessie. "I understand you are from America."

"That's right," said Jessie. "My name is Jessica Adams. And this is my niece, Katherine Thompson."

"James explained that you need a place to stay. He knows that on occasion I rent out a room," explained Mrs. Dawson. "Only to respectable women, of course," she quickly added.

Jessie spoke in her most ladylike manner. "Would you be willing to let us stay for a night or two? We would try not to be a bother."

"I should be pleased," said Mrs. Dawson. "Indeed, you are welcome to come with me now. My carriage is just outside."

With another farewell to James, Mrs. Dawson sailed toward the door. Kat and Jessie trailed along behind her—murmuring their thanks to James as they did so.

Outside, Mrs. Dawson led them to an open carriage. A tired-looking, gray-haired man sat in the driver's seat. He held the reins of two horses—also tired and gray.

"We have some new lodgers, Thomas," said Mrs. Dawson. "From America."

"Wonderful, madam," said Thomas as he stepped down from his seat. He helped Mrs. Dawson into the carriage, then Jessie. Kat hopped up on her own, earning a wink and a smile.

Soon they were off, dodging carriages, children, and people selling everything from lemonade to dog collars. Kat stared about in fascination as she listened to Mrs. Dawson.

"America! That is such a long way to come. My daughter

and her husband live there now in New York City. They rarely make it back to England."

"Have you ever visited them there?" asked Jessie.

"Heavens no!" said Mrs. Dawson. "And I have no intention of making such a long ocean voyage. Though I admire you for being so daring," she added.

Kat gasped as she caught sight of a magnificent building. Mrs. Dawson noticed and smiled. "Westminster Palace," she announced proudly. "It was completed just last year."

She began to point out other sights. They crossed the Thames River, which was thick with boats. Then the carriage wound its way through a beautiful park and past another grand building.

"That is Buckingham Palace," noted Mrs. Dawson. "Home of Queen Victoria and Prince Albert and their dear children."

For Kat, the ride came to an end all too soon. They stopped in front of a lovely—if slightly run-down— three-story house. It was connected to the houses on either side. In fact, houses formed a row of brick that stretched all the way down the street.

"Come along," said Mrs. Dawson. "We must get you settled." She marched up the steps and into the house with Kat and Jessie in tow.

As Kat's eyes grew used to the dim light inside, she stared about in amazement. Every surface was covered. Shelves and tables held glass dishes and china statues. A flowered silk cloth was draped across a grand piano. Circlets of fancy lace protected the backs and arms of every chair. And the flowered wallpaper was almost hidden behind dozens of small pictures.

Before Kat could take it all in, a girl about her own age

appeared. She wore a simple dress with a white apron tied at the waist. "Good day, Mrs. Dawson," the girl said with a curtsy.

"Lucy," said Mrs. Dawson with a nod. "We have some lodgers from America. Miss Adams and her niece, Katherine Thompson. Please show them to the spare room."

Lucy's eyes lit up, and she broke into a smile. Kat couldn't help smiling back.

"From America!" said Lucy. "That's a wonder, for sure!" Then, remembering her task, she turned serious. "This way, ladies. I'll carry your bag."

Traveling bag in hand, Lucy led them up a long staircase. Mrs. Dawson's voice floated up behind them. "When you are settled, come down for a bit of dinner."

Lucy made her way to the end of a narrow hall and pushed open a door. "This is your room," she said, placing the traveling bag on a low dresser. "The bed is all made up for you. I'll bring you some things for washing up. And I'll have dinner ready soon."

Jessie and Kat thanked the girl.

When they were alone, Kat asked, "Who do you think she is, Jessie? Surely she's not Mrs. Dawson's daughter."

"Oh no," replied Jessie. "I'm certain she's a servant."

"But she's only about my age," protested Kat. "And it sounds like she does all the work around here!"

"You're probably right about that," said Jessie. "From the look of things, Mrs. Dawson isn't exactly well-off. So she'd hardly have a house full of servants. You can see that everything is tidy but worn." She pointed toward the coverlet on the bed, which was faded and neatly patched.

"Now before I do anything else," said Jessie, "I need to be able to breathe."

Kat laughed. "I'll help."

And Jessie needed Kat's help. Her dress had dozens of tiny buttons down the front. Once those were undone, Kat untied the laces of the corset underneath.

Jessie took a deep breath. "Thank goodness!" she sighed. "I never truly appreciated modern clothing until now!"

Kat helped her lace up the corset again—but much more loosely. By the time Jessie had done up the buttons of her dress, Lucy was back. She carried a pitcher of warm water, soap, and a towel.

As she poured the water into a bowl on the washstand, Lucy glanced at them. "If you don't mind my asking, is this your first visit to London?"

Jessie shook her head. "No, I was here once before. Several years ago." Then she frowned as she got tangled up in the sense of her remark. Her earlier visit hadn't really been several years in the past. It had been far in the future!

"And you, Miss Katherine?"

"Oh no. I've never been here before. But please, call me Kat."

"That'd hardly be proper," said Lucy. "Mrs. Dawson'd have a fit if she heard."

"Well then, we won't let her hear," said Kat.

Jessie laughed. "By all means, Lucy, call her Kat. And call me Jessie. I'll explain to Mrs. Dawson that that's the way things are done in America."

At that, Lucy laughed too. "She won't be surprised," she said. "Mrs. Dawson is sure that American manners aren't what

29

they should be." Then she added, "I'd love to see it, though. America, I mean."

She sighed, "But I'm talking too much. I'd best get back to work."

As Lucy left the room, Jessie glanced at the traveling bag. "Maybe we should put that out of sight, Kat," she suggested.

"Good idea," said Kat. "And the encyclopedia." Kat loosened the drawstring of her purse and pulled out the book. "I'll put them together in the closet," she said.

Kat opened the big leather bag to put the encyclopedia inside. But her hand froze, and she stared down in shock.

"No!" she cried. "It can't be!"

The Wrong Bag

W hat's the matter?" Jessie asked as she hurried to Kat's side.

Without answering, Kat pointed to the bag. Jessie looked inside and gasped. "What's going on? What is all that stuff doing in our bag?"

"I don't know," groaned Kat. She pushed aside a man's shirt, dark jacket, and pair of trousers.

Jessie sat down heavily on a nearby chair. In a dull voice, she said, "It's not our bag, is it?"

"No, I'm afraid not," said Kat.

"So the time machine isn't there, is it?" added Jessie.

"No," repeated Kat, her voice thick with misery. She knew that the same terrible thought had occurred to both of them. Without the machine, they'd never get back to their own time.

Jessie rose to her feet. "How could this have happened?"

"I must have picked up the wrong bag," Kat admitted. "But I don't see how I could have done that. It was beside me the whole time we were in the station!"

"Okay, let's stay calm and think things through," said Jessie. She began to pace. "I know I put the bag down while I looked through the encyclopedia."

"That's right," said Kat. "But it was right at my feet. I checked. And I grabbed it when—"

31

She stopped, a look of horror on her face.

"What is it?" asked Jessie. "Do you know what happened to the bag?"

"I'm not sure," said Kat. "But there was this man standing next to me. I noticed him because he was so tall. And because he was almost completely bald. I remember the way the light bounced off his head."

She continued. "He had a bag just like ours. I saw him put it on the floor. I must have grabbed his bag when a crowd of people started toward me."

"Then he probably has our bag," Jessie said. "Well, we'll have to find out who he is and trade bags. Let's check for a tag of some kind."

But the stranger's name wasn't anywhere on the bag.

"Now what?" asked Kat.

"I hate to go through someone else's belongings. But I guess that's what we're going to have to do."

So they looked at each item. This time they had a little more luck. In a jacket pocket, Kat found some English pound notes and a ticket.

Kat read the words on the ticket aloud. "'Season ticket of admission to the Exhibition of the Works of Industry of All Nations, 1851.'"

She added, "There's a space for the ticket-holder's name. But he didn't sign it."

"Great," muttered Jessie. She was still looking through the bag. "Kat, there's something else in here."

She pulled out a heavy spring with square plates of metal attached to both ends. There were holes in each corner of the plates.

"What can that be?" asked Kat.

"Maybe this will tell us something about it," said Jessie. She removed several sheets of writing paper from the bag.

Kat and Jessie bent over the top sheet. In the center of the page was a sketch of a rectangular object. It appeared to have legs at both ends and a V-shaped support in the middle. But the oddest thing was the clock shown at one end of the rectangle. Near this was an arrow pointing to the legs and the words "Fold here."

"Does any of this make sense to you?" asked Kat.

Jessie shook her head. "The owner of the bag is obviously here for the exhibition. So I'd guess that this is a plan for an invention. But I can't figure out what it's supposed to do."

She turned the paper over. "Here's an enlarged drawing of one part of the invention."

"Wait just a minute!" cried Kat, pointing at the sketch. "Doesn't this look a little like the gizmo we found in the bag?"

Sure enough, the sketch did look like the strange metal object. Except that in the sketch, a thick rope was shown in place of the spring.

"So the gizmo must be part of a larger machine," murmured Jessie.

"And look," Kat added. "The word 'Strand' is written here. That must have something to do with the piece of rope."

Jessie bent closer. "It's hard to tell," she said. "The paper is ripped right above the word."

"Okay," said Kat. "So we can't figure out what the invention is. That's not what's really important anyway. How about the other piece of paper? What does it say?"

Jessie glanced at the second sheet. "It's a letter," she reported. "Maybe it'll give us a clue about the owner."

Kat leaned over Jessie's shoulder so they could both read.

> Edward,
>
> Your ticket to the exhibition is enclosed, and I await your arrival. This event is truly our chance to make a name for ourselves. Our sponsor assures me that the prince has promised to come by our exhibit sometime soon after the opening. As usual, the press will be with him. We must quickly add the device you are bringing so that our marvelous invention will work properly. I know it will be a great success. Our fortune will be made, and the family estate will be saved.
>
> Your brother,
> Sidney

"Wouldn't you know it—he's writing to his brother. So he doesn't sign his last name!" complained Jessie. "If only we had the envelope the letter came in."

She sighed. "Still, we have learned something. The owner of the bag will be at the exhibition."

"We've learned something else too," added Kat gloomily. "We know that without this part, the brothers' invention won't work."

She moaned. "Oh, Jessie. I've ruined everything! I managed to lose the time machine and get us stuck here in the past. And I've ruined the brothers' chance at success! Maybe their last chance!"

CHAPTER SIX

Lucy's London

A knock kept Jessie from responding. She opened the door to find Lucy standing outside.

"Dinner's ready," Lucy announced.

"Thank you," replied Jessie.

With troubled minds, they followed Lucy down to the dining room. Mrs. Dawson stood waiting beside a table set with china and polished silverware. "I expect you are hungry after your trip," she said. She motioned them to their chairs.

As they settled into their seats, Lucy disappeared. She was back in a few moments with a platter of grayish meat. She set this in front of Mrs. Dawson. On another trip, she brought back several steaming bowls.

"You must have some stewed beef," Mrs. Dawson said to Jessie, passing her the platter. "And Lucy has a way with turnips," she added as she passed a bowl.

Kat hated turnips, but felt she had to take some. The beef didn't look tempting either. It was stringy and shapeless, as though it had been cooked for days. But nothing would have pleased Kat tonight. Her worries had killed her appetite.

As she tried to eat, Kat only half listened to Mrs. Dawson. She really didn't need to pay close attention anyway. Most of the woman's remarks were directed toward Jessie.

"The exhibition is said to be quite wonderful," Mrs. Dawson was saying. "Why, there are thousands of exhibitors! One can see marvels from all around the world."

Mrs. Dawson went on and on. But finally she noticed that her guests were doing more rearranging of their food than actual eating. "Ladies, you hardly seem to be enjoying your dinner! What is the matter—if I may ask?"

Kat and Jessie exchanged a long look. Finally Jessie sighed. "Please forgive me, Mrs. Dawson. Everything is quite tasty. And we appreciate your kindness. It's just that we've discovered that we have a problem."

"Well, then," said Mrs. Dawson in a firm voice. "We shall have to discover a solution."

Jessie smiled at that. "You're absolutely right. It doesn't do much good to waste time worrying. You see, there's been a mix-up. We've lost our traveling bag. And the one we have belongs to someone else."

"How dreadful," said Mrs. Dawson. Yet Kat noticed that she seemed more excited than upset. "Why, you only had one bag. So this means you have none of your things with you!"

At once she plucked a silver bell from the table and rang it. "I will see that this is taken care of immediately."

Lucy arrived almost before the ringing faded away. "Yes, ma'am?" she asked.

"Lucy!" trumpeted Mrs. Dawson. "Our guests have lost their luggage. They are going to need nightclothes. As soon as you are done in the kitchen, please look through the chest in the attic. I am sure we can find something there that will do."

36

"Yes, ma'am," nodded Lucy before hurrying off.

"There's no need to go to any trouble," Jessie said. "It's not losing our clothing that's the real problem."

"Then what is?" asked Mrs. Dawson.

"We had something very important in our bag," Jessie replied. "Something we must get back."

"Oh?" said Mrs. Dawson. Clearly she was waiting to be told what the "important" thing was. However, when Jessie didn't offer that information, Mrs. Dawson went on.

"I know just what to do. Tomorrow I will send Thomas back to the railway station. He can check to see if your bag was turned in. And he can inquire at the police station as well. After that—"

Kat couldn't remain quiet any longer. "I'm sorry, Mrs. Dawson, but there's another problem. The other bag belongs to someone who is displaying an invention at the exhibition. And there's something in there that he needs right away."

This new wrinkle didn't stop Mrs. Dawson for long. "All the more reason to send Thomas to the station," she said. "He can see if the owner of the other bag has asked about it. If not, I think you should put a notice in the *Times*. Since you say it is a gentleman's bag you have, that may work," she added. "No lady would read the *Times*. The news is much too shocking."

Jessie smiled. "Thank you for your suggestions, Mrs. Dawson. I feel better. However, Thomas doesn't have to do anything. Kat and I can take care of this."

"Nonsense," replied Mrs. Dawson. "Thomas will be glad to help."

Kat couldn't help wondering if Thomas would feel the same way. Still, she had to admit that she too felt better. Mrs. Dawson was obviously not one to let problems go unsolved.

Suddenly Kat felt hungry. She happily finished up her dinner—turnips and all.

Satisfied that she had things under control, Mrs. Dawson returned to her earlier topic. She told them about the years of planning that had gone into the Great Exhibition. She spoke of Prince Albert's role in starting the project. And she talked about the huge building that housed the exhibits—the Crystal Palace.

Lucy, who had come to clear away plates, spoke up. "It's a grand sight!"

Mrs. Dawson stared at the girl in surprise. "Why, Lucy, when did you see the Crystal Palace?"

Lucy blushed. "I've been walking that way some days before I go home, ma'am. I wanted to see what it was like."

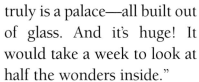

She turned to Kat and Jessie. "It truly is a palace—all built out of glass. And it's huge! It would take a week to look at half the wonders inside."

With that, Lucy gathered up the rest of the dishes and left the room. Mrs. Dawson gazed after her. "My goodness," she said. "Hyde Park is a bit out of the way for Lucy, I believe. I am surprised that she would bother to walk that far."

"I think she's like me," suggested Kat. "I'm curious about everything too."

"Curious?" repeated Mrs. Dawson. "Hmmm, I suppose Lucy *is* curious. I've certainly heard her asking Thomas enough questions about places he has been."

"Lucy said she went to see the Crystal Palace on her way

home," said Kat. "Where does she live?"

"Why...I have no idea, Katherine," said Mrs. Dawson. "Somewhere near Covent Garden, I believe. At least her cousin lives in that area, I know."

When Kat looked confused, Mrs. Dawson explained. "Lucy's cousin works for an old friend of mine. On occasion Lucy went in as day help there. So when I was looking for a maid-of-all-work, my friend suggested her."

Kat couldn't understand why Mrs. Dawson wasn't more interested in Lucy's life. There was so much she wanted to know about the girl, and they'd only just met. However, she realized that if she wanted information, she'd probably have to talk to Lucy.

But Kat didn't see Lucy again that evening. When she asked about her, she was told that Lucy had gone home.

At last Jessie excused herself and Kat. "We're tired from our long trip," she explained. "And we have a lot to do tomorrow."

"I understand," said Mrs. Dawson. "Sleep well, Miss Adams. And you too, Katherine."

Despite Mrs. Dawson's good wishes, neither Kat nor Jessie could get to sleep right away. Dressed in the nightclothes they found laid out for them, they lay in bed and talked. They agreed that they'd try everything Mrs. Dawson had suggested. Surely they would find the inventor—and their own bag.

As exciting as this trip was, they had no desire to remain in London forever. But right now, home seemed impossibly far away.

~

"You said you wanted to solve your own problem," Mrs. Dawson commented the next morning. "I can understand that. I am the same way. So Thomas will take you to the train station, Miss Adams. Then, if need be, you can go on to the police station. And to the offices of the *Times* as well."

"Should I come with you?" Kat asked Jessie.

Mrs. Dawson looked horrified. "Heavens, Katherine. It is bad enough that your aunt must go to such places. Certainly you—a mere child—should not."

"Why don't you stay here, Kat," suggested Jessie. "I'm sure you can help Lucy."

Kat brightened. She would enjoy spending some time with Lucy and learning about her life.

But Mrs. Dawson started to sputter. "Really, Miss Adams. It is not Katherine's place to help Lucy. It would never do."

Jessie flashed a warm smile. "Forgive me," she said. "It's just that, in America, Kat is used to helping around the house. And she would enjoy being with Lucy—someone her own age. Besides, she wants to learn about life here in England."

Mrs. Dawson turned thoughtful. "I see your point," she said. "Traveling should be an educational experience. And you will be using the carriage. So I have no way to show Katherine around the city myself."

She thought for another moment. "Perhaps she should go with Lucy to Covent Garden. She will find that a most interesting experience. And Lucy must go there anyway to do the day's marketing."

"That's an excellent idea," murmured Jessie. "And most educational, I am sure. Now, if you will excuse me?" She winked at Kat, then went outside where Thomas waited with the carriage.

Mrs. Dawson quickly summoned Lucy. "Are you ready to go to the market?" she asked.

"Yes, I am," replied Lucy. "I've just finished the morning's dusting, ma'am."

"Well, Miss Adams and I feel that Katherine should see Covent Garden. So she will be coming with you."

Kat smiled when she saw the pleased look on Lucy's face. The girl bobbed a quick curtsy. "I'd be happy to show her around."

"Very well," said Mrs. Dawson. "You might as well be off."

Together the two girls set out. The missing bag was still on Kat's mind—as was the fear of being stuck forever in the past. Even so, it was impossible for her not to be excited about this adventure.

"Can I ask you some questions?" she asked Lucy.

"Of course," replied Lucy with a laugh.

"Where do you live," asked Kat. "What's your family like? Why do you have to work?" She paused for breath, then turned red.

"I'm sorry, Lucy," she added quietly. "I sound like a real busybody."

Lucy laughed again. "I don't mind," she said. "I guess I'm one too. So when I'm done answering your questions, I'll ask you some of my own."

"It's a deal," agreed Kat.

"I live right near Covent Garden," said Lucy. "As for my family, there's just me, my mum, and my little brother, Ned."

"What happened to—" Kat stopped. Maybe she shouldn't ask.

"To my father?" guessed Lucy. "He died a couple years back. He worked in the coal mines before we came to London. Took in too much black dust, Mum says. It was his chest that killed him."

"I'm sorry," said Kat softly.

Lucy shrugged. "I'm luckier than most girls my age. I miss him, mind you. But at least I've got Mum and Ned."

She added, "As to why I work, Mum can't support us on her own. And it's a good job I've got."

"But you have to do everything!" protested Kat. "And Mrs. Dawson is so—so bossy!"

"Ah, she's not that bad," said Lucy. "There are worse jobs, believe me. Mrs. Dawson's never raised a hand to me. She gives me some of her daughter's old clothes so Mum can cut them down for me. And she lets me eat all I want. No, I've no complaints."

Kat felt a touch of shame. I moan and groan when it's my turn to do the dishes, she thought.

"Now tell me about your home and family," said Lucy. So Kat did—as well as she could without revealing that both were far in the future.

By the time she finished her story, they had reached Covent Garden. Kat was a bit surprised to find that it looked nothing like a garden. In fact, it was a huge paved square packed with people. Some drove carts and wagons loaded with fruits and vegetables. Others carried brimming baskets on their heads. All were headed toward a huge barn-like building at the center of the square.

"That's the market," explained Lucy, pointing to the building.

"But why is it called a garden?" asked Kat.

"There used to be one here, hundreds of years ago," explained Lucy. "This is where the rich once

lived. I read about it in—" she paused, looking worried.

"Where did you read about it?" asked Kat.

"Ummm...Well, it was in a book of Mrs. Dawson's. When I was dusting," Lucy admitted. She went on in a rush. "I love to read, and I've no books at home. So I like to hurry through the dusting and then sneak in a bit of reading."

Kat thought about how awful she'd feel if there were no books in her home.

"How did you learn to read, Lucy?" Kat asked. "I mean, if you don't have any books at home?"

"Mum knows how, and she taught me," replied Lucy. "The two of us read anything—even the newspapers the fish seller wraps fish in!"

Kat had to smile at that. "I'm the same way," she said. "And I've gotten in trouble for reading when I was supposed to be doing something else."

They made their way into the market building. Merchants were everywhere with their goods set out before them.

The first thing Kat noticed was the smell. The scent of onions mixed with that of ripe strawberries. And over the good smells were the unmistakable odors of unwashed bodies and horse manure.

"Let me get the marketing done first," said Lucy. "Then we can explore a bit."

Lucy quickly went from stall to stall. Sometimes she passed by without a word. Other times she stopped and bartered with the merchants.

In short order, Lucy had filled her basket. "Two turnips, a head of cabbage, and some potatoes," she said. "That should do. The strawberries are still too dear."

"What do you mean by 'too dear'?" asked Kat.

"They cost too much," said Lucy simply. "Mrs. Dawson has enough to get by. But I know she has to watch her money. So I try to get the best bargains for her."

The shopping finished, Kat and Lucy wandered through the market. The sights and sounds overwhelmed Kat. It reminded her of going to the mall in late December, when the stores were packed.

But it must be like that every day of the year here, thought Kat.

Lucy, who had been quiet for a while, looked at Kat thoughtfully. "Would you like to meet my mum?" she asked.

Kat broke into a smile. "I'd love to!"

"Come on, then," said Lucy. She led the way out of the market building and across the square. There stood a row of ten or more women. Their dresses were patched and worn, but their baskets of flowers were lovely. "Sweet violets," they called to passersby. "Roses for your lady love."

"There's Mum," Lucy said, nodding to a woman near the end of the row. Kat found it hard to guess the woman's age. Her long brown hair was faded, and her thin face was lined.

At the sight of Lucy, a smile lit up the woman's face. "Lucy, love," she greeted her daughter. "Are you doing Mrs. Dawson's marketing?"

"I am, Mum. I just finished. And I wanted you to meet someone. This is Miss Katherine Thompson. She's lodging with Mrs. Dawson for a bit. She's come all the way from America."

"From America," echoed the woman. She nodded to Kat. "I'm Edith Green, Miss Thompson," she said. "Pleased to meet you."

"Call me Kat. I've managed to get Lucy to do that. And I'd

like you to as well."

Mrs. Green smiled. "I will, Kat. Though I wonder how Mrs. Dawson feels about such a thing."

She glanced at her daughter, who started to laugh. "Don't worry, Mum," Lucy assured her. "She hasn't heard me do it."

Kat added, "She considers Americans strange anyway. So I wouldn't worry too much about it."

"Well, Kat, welcome to London," Mrs. Green said. She waved her hand toward the marketplace. "I think this is one of the finest sights in the whole city. I'm glad Lucy's brought you to see it."

"It *is* wonderful," said Kat.

"Now before you run off, I've something for you," Mrs. Green remarked. She plucked a bunch of purple violets from her basket and handed them to Kat.

Murmuring her thanks, Kat took the flowers and sniffed their sweet scent. As she lifted her head, she caught sight of a large poster. It hung on the wall of the building behind the flower sellers. And there was a familiar word on it.

Just then the large lady next to Mrs. Green moved and blocked part of the poster. Kat quickly stepped back to get a clearer view.

"Kat, look out!" warned Lucy.

At the same time, a rough voice called, "Watch it, miss!"

Kat spun around. But it was too late. A large, wheeled cart was headed right for her!

CHAPTER SEVEN

The Missing Strand

Kat jumped to the side just in time. But she tripped over her long skirts and went down in a heap on the pavement.

"Kat!" cried Lucy.

"Dear me!" exclaimed Mrs. Green.

The man who'd been pushing the cart pulled it to a halt. Several muffins tumbled from the cart to the ground.

"I'm sorry, miss," he said as he helped Kat to her feet. "But you stepped right in front of me."

"It was my fault," said Kat. "I'll pay you for the muffins that fell."

"Don't trouble yourself about that," said the muffin man. "They're still fit to sell." He dusted the muffins off on his dirty apron, then plopped them back on the cart.

"If you're all right, I'd best be on me way." He tipped his hat and added, "Again, sorry about the upset, miss."

As the man hurried off, Lucy gasped. "Kat! You're hurt!"

Kat glanced down and saw that the sleeve of her dress was torn. And there was a big scrape on her elbow. Only now did it start to tingle and burn.

"We'd better get that taken care of," said Mrs. Green. She turned to her daughter. "Lucy, I must stay here if I hope to sell anything today. But you can stop at home and help Kat get that elbow cleaned up."

"There's no need to do that," protested Kat. "It's not that serious."

But Mrs. Green insisted. So Lucy led Kat out of the square and down a nearby street. From there they stepped into a narrow alley lined with tall buildings.

High overhead, women leaned out windows. Some talked to their neighbors on the other side of the alley. Some hung clothing from lines that stretched across the empty space. Several called greetings to Lucy.

"Here we go," said Lucy, pointing at a stairway that led down. Kat followed her into a small room.

Kat couldn't help staring around curiously. She noted that a few wooden chairs and a table took up much of the floor space. In the far corner, a tattered blanket formed a divider. Kat could see a mattress just behind. A small fireplace, now cold, took up half of one wall.

Is this it? thought Kat. Is this how Lucy lives?

"Well, let's get you cleaned up," Lucy said. Businesslike, she moved to the table and poured water from a cracked pitcher into a bowl. "Take a seat," she said, pointing to a chair.

In no time, Lucy had gently washed and wrapped Kat's elbow. "There," she said. "That'll do till we get to Mrs. Dawson's."

While Lucy had acted as nurse, Kat had taken a closer look at the room. As small as the place was, there were many touches that made it a home. A jug of violets sat in

the middle of the table. Several black-and-white prints were tacked on the walls. Across the arm of a rocking chair, a faded blanket lay in neat folds. And a small wooden horse sat next to Kat's chair.

The horse made Kat think about the little brother Lucy had mentioned. He hadn't been with Lucy's mother. So she asked, "Lucy, where's Ned?"

"Oh, he's off at ragged school."

"Ragged school?" repeated Kat.

"It's for poor folks like us," said Lucy matter-of-factly. "It doesn't cost anything to go there. It's not much of a school, really. But it's better than no school at all."

"If it's free, can't you go too?" Kat asked.

"Me?" replied Lucy. "I've no time for such things, Kat. We need the money I earn. Besides, there's little reason for a girl to go."

That brought Kat up short. But then she remembered that this was the nineteenth century. From history class, she knew that Lucy was saying what many people of the time believed.

I'm glad I'm only visiting, Kat thought. At least I hope I'm only visiting.

She stood up and thanked Lucy for bandaging her arm. Then she remembered what she'd seen at the market.

"Lucy, I almost forgot!" she said. "There was a poster on the wall behind your mother. I was trying to read it when I stepped into the muffin man's way."

"What did it say?" asked Lucy.

"It was about a play, I think. And the poster said that the theater was 'off the Strand.'"

"That's right," replied Lucy. "There's a grand theater there. Do you want to see the play?"

"No, that's not what got my attention," said Kat. "It was the bit about the Strand. Is it a street?"

"Why, yes," said Lucy. "And not too far from the market."

Kat grinned. "I was right! This could be a clue!"

Lucy gave her a puzzled look. She knew about the bag mix-up and the piece of the invention. But she hadn't heard about the sketch. So Kat quickly filled her in.

"You see, the paper was ripped just above the word 'Strand,'" Kat finished. "Maybe the word had nothing to do with the invention. Maybe it was part of a street address. The inventor might be staying there while he's in London."

Lucy caught Kat's excitement. "There's more than one lodging house along the Strand," she said. "It's a likely enough place for a visitor to stay."

"Great," said Kat. "Jessie and I can scout around."

"I know those parts pretty well," said Lucy. "Why don't we try now? The Strand's just down the way."

Kat quickly agreed. A short walk took them the few blocks to the Strand. There Lucy led the way to a large lodging house.

"I worked for the landlady here a day or two in the past," she explained. "I'm sure she'll help you if I ask."

However, after Lucy had explained things, the woman shook her head. "I've no new lodgers, Lucy," she said. "All my gentlemen have been here for ages."

But she was able to tell them of several other lodging houses down the street. And she was sure that some were offering rooms to exhibition visitors.

So the girls visited two more houses. At each one, Kat described the tall, thin, balding man she'd seen. She explained that his first name was probably Edward. At each house, she was told that there was no such lodger.

Their fourth stop brought them to a shabby brick building. After a while, their knock was answered by a man who looked equally shabby.

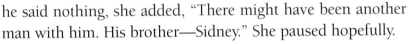

He listened as Kat gave her description of the inventor. When he said nothing, she added, "There might have been another man with him. His brother—Sidney." She paused hopefully.

The man scratched his chin and eyed Kat. "Bald, you say? No one comes to mind, miss. No Edward or Sidney, either. Of course, my memory isn't always what it ought to be," he added. He gave her a foxy smile and stood there, obviously waiting for something.

Lucy leaned over. "A halfpence might help his memory," she whispered.

Sure enough, as soon as Kat handed over the coppery coin, the man smiled. "Ah yes. It's coming back now," he remarked. "A balding man. One did stay here last night. And you're right. He was with another man—his brother. Both of them inventors, he said."

"Are they here now?" asked Kat. "May we speak to them?"

The man smoothed his thick mustache before answering. "They're gone," he finally admitted.

Lucy broke in, "When will they be back?"

"Well, they won't be," he replied. "Seems they'd come on hard times. Could barely pay me one night's lodging. So they left this morning."

"No!" cried Kat. "Do you know where they went?"

"I don't," said the man. "Though I ought to remember their names. Let me see..."

At Lucy's nudge, Kat handed over another coin.

"Barrington! That was it!" he announced.

Kat soon realized he had nothing more to offer. So she and Lucy said their good-byes and hurried down the steps.

Kat paused there to think. "Knowing their name may help," she said. "I need to talk to Jessie. Let's go back to Mrs. Dawson's."

"Mrs. Dawson!" moaned Lucy with a look of horror. "Oh, mercy! I've forgotten all about what I was supposed to be doing. I'll catch it for sure for taking so long to do the marketing!"

"Come on," said Kat, grabbing Lucy's hand. "We'll hurry. And I'll explain that it's my fault you're late."

The girls ran all the way back to the house. They dashed into the kitchen to find Mrs. Dawson waiting there, a frown on her face. "Lucy! Where have you been?" she demanded. "I've been worried."

Then she caught sight of Kat's elbow. "Katherine, you are injured!" she exclaimed. Shaking her head, Mrs. Dawson turned to Lucy. "I trusted you to take care of our visitor, Lucy. This is absolutely dreadful!"

CHAPTER EIGHT

The Grand & Glorious Exhibition

Kat waited for Lucy to explain. But the other girl merely said, "I'm sorry, ma'am. Both for being late and for what happened to Miss Katherine. I'd best get on with my work now." With a nod toward Kat, she disappeared into the pantry.

Mrs. Dawson stared after the girl for a moment. Then she turned and left the kitchen.

Kat didn't hesitate. "Mrs. Dawson! Wait!" she called.

Mrs. Dawson stopped so suddenly that her wide skirt swung like a bell. "What is it, Katherine?" she asked.

"It wasn't Lucy's fault we were so late, ma'am. It was mine," said Kat. She added, "Please don't be angry with her."

"Really, my dear child. I think I know what is best for Lucy. A firm hand—"

"But Lucy tries so hard to do a good job," Kat dared to interrupt.

Now the older woman looked shocked. "Why, I am aware of that, Katherine. And heaven knows, I appreciate the child. Has she said something that would make you think otherwise?"

"No, of course not," said Kat. "It's just..."

"Yes?" prompted Mrs. Dawson.

"It's just that everything is so hard for Lucy, don't you see?"

"I hardly think Lucy is overworked here," said Mrs.

53

Dawson, her eyes snapping.

"Oh, I didn't mean that either. I don't know how to explain what I *do* mean!" cried Kat.

Mrs. Dawson noted Kat's flushed cheeks, and her glance softened. "Come into the parlor, Katherine. Perhaps if we sit down, you can explain your thoughts in a clearer fashion."

So Kat found herself perched on the edge of a large chair. Mrs. Dawson sat across from her, hands neatly folded.

The story spilled out of Kat. She started by explaining about her accident and why they were so late. Then she told about how hard Lucy's mother worked and how little the family had. She also mentioned Lucy's struggle to see that her brother went to school. And how happy Lucy was to have a job with Mrs. Dawson.

When Kat finished, Mrs. Dawson remained silent, staring at her own hands. Finally she raised her eyes.

"Are things different in America, Katherine?" she asked. "For those who are less fortunate than you?"

It was Kat's turn to fall silent. Were things much different in America in 1851? She wasn't sure. But she remembered reading stories about children who worked in mills. Or worse yet, were slaves.

"I guess not," she admitted.

"It speaks well of you to care so much, my dear," said Mrs. Dawson. "And I will admit, I had given little thought to Lucy's home life. I believed I knew everything I needed to know about her. Perhaps not. It seems she has been a mystery to me."

"She's not really such a mystery," Kat assured her. "In fact, she's a lot like me. We're both curious about things—a lot of things. We like exploring. And we both love to read more than anything else."

"Lucy likes to read?" asked Mrs. Dawson.

"Yes, ma'am," said Kat. Suddenly she realized that she probably shouldn't have said anything. Would Mrs. Dawson be angry if she knew Lucy read her books?

"It never occurred to me that she would know how," murmured Mrs. Dawson. "I cannot imagine—"

She broke off as a knock came at the parlor door. It was Thomas—with Jessie right behind. He bowed Jessie into the room, then went back to see to the horses.

"Any luck?" Kat asked.

"No," sighed Jessie. "No one has turned in our bag at the train station. And the police couldn't do much to help. Given the exhibition crowds, they simply have too much to deal with.

"The last place Thomas took me was to the newspaper offices," she added. "I paid for a notice in the *Times*. But it won't appear for several days."

"Well, Lucy and I found out something," Kat announced. "We know the inventors' last name is Barrington."

Kat told her story again. Then she added, "I bet that someone at the exhibition will be able to tell us where to find them. In fact, I was hoping we could go to the Crystal Palace right away to check it out."

Mrs. Dawson drew back. "My dear, there are thousands and thousands of displays. How can you hope to find one exhibitor? Besides, this is the very first week of the exhibition. It will be impossibly crowded!"

Jessie shook her head. "It will probably be as bad as you say, Mrs. Dawson. But we don't have any other hope. Neither do the Barringtons. Not if they want to finish their machine before the prince visits."

"Very well," said Mrs. Dawson. "If you are set on going, I

want Thomas to take you there."

"Thank you," said Jessie. "You're very kind."

"Nonsense," said Mrs. Dawson. "And once you have straightened out the bags, have a wonderful time. This is the most glorious event ever to take place in England!"

The pride in Mrs. Dawson's voice brought a smile to Jessie's face. "I'm sure you'll enjoy the exhibition when you go yourself," she said.

"Oh...perhaps later," said Mrs. Dawson quietly. "Not at first. Not when the tickets are so—"

Kat knew what Mrs. Dawson was too proud to say. That the tickets were too expensive. She remembered what she'd read on the posters at the train station. Tickets cost much more now than they would later.

Kat looked at her aunt, a plea in her eyes. "Jessie," she said. "I'm a little worried. There are so many exhibits. Maybe it would be better if we had some help."

"Help?" began Jessie. But she quickly realized what Kat was trying to say. "I see what you mean," she said.

She turned to Mrs. Dawson. "You've been so kind that I hate to ask for another favor. But would you be willing to come to the exhibition with us? As our guest, of course. Having three sets of eyes would be such a help."

"Come with you?" echoed Mrs. Dawson. "Why... Why...Why, certainly!" She broke into a broad smile. "You are quite right to ask. I am sure I can be of help to you."

～

In short order, the three of them were in the carriage, headed for Hyde Park. As they neared the park, Kat leaned

56

forward eagerly. At first she saw only trees and acres of thick, green grass. Then a small lake appeared. And there on the opposite bank stood a huge structure. It seemed to be made entirely of sparkling glass.

"The Crystal Palace," sighed Mrs. Dawson. "It truly is marvelous."

Thomas guided the carriage over a bridge that crossed the lake. As they drew nearer, Kat saw that iron frames supported the sheets of glass. The building rose three stories high—even higher with the barrel-shaped arch in the center.

Thomas drove them the entire length of the Crystal Palace to the main entrance. He let them off there with a promise to return in several hours.

After buying tickets and a catalog of the exhibits, Jessie led the way inside. Kat took three steps and then stopped, stunned. The inside was even more amazing than the outside. In the center of the entry hall stood a fountain of pure crystal. Wide staircases led up to railed walkways that ran along the upper level of the building. And near the entrance, three elm trees towered overhead.

"How did they ever get those trees in here?" Kat asked.

"They built the palace around them," Mrs. Dawson said. "The original plans called for cutting the trees down, but the people of London refused to let that happen. So the design was changed to fit them."

Kat lowered her gaze and stared down the packed hall. Mrs. Dawson had been right about the crowds. People were every-where—talking, laughing, pushing past. How would they ever find the two men they were looking for? Even if they did know their names.

"Where do we start?" she asked.

Jessie looked up from the catalog. "There's a map here. It seems the exhibits are arranged by country. So I suggest we start with the displays from England. That's the largest section anyway," she added. "Besides, it has something called the 'Machinery Court.' "

"And we're pretty sure the brothers are exhibiting some kind of machine," said Kat.

"Lead the way," ordered Mrs. Dawson, sounding as if she were ready for battle. She gave a wave of her folded umbrella, which she clutched as usual.

Jessie herded them toward the west wing of the palace. It proved slow going. Not only were the halls packed, but it was hard to hurry by some of the exhibits.

Kat had to stop to look at something called a "ventilating hat." It had holes that could be opened or closed depending on how hot the wearer's head was.

Jessie was entranced by a model of the solar system. A clever system of gears made the planets move around the sun.

And Mrs. Dawson came to a complete standstill in front of a display of small animals. All had been stuffed and arranged into scenes. A white rat served as schoolmaster to a mouse and some rabbits. Another mouse played a piano.

"How charming," said Mrs. Dawson. "They would be just delightful in my parlor." Kat shuddered at the thought. Imagine having to look at such a thing every day!

In between examining exhibits, they searched the crowd. But the man from the train station was nowhere to be seen.

At last they heard the humming, pounding, and thumping of many machines. Devices of all shapes and sizes filled every inch of the exhibit area. They had arrived at the Machinery Court.

Jessie approached an exhibitor. "Excuse me," she said over the noise. "Do you know where Sidney and Edward Barrington might be exhibiting?"

"No, miss," he replied. "I've never heard of them."

They received similar answers as they made their way down the line of exhibits.

Finally a young man who was passing by overheard. "Pardon me," he said, tipping his hat to Jessie. "I couldn't help but hear. You are looking for the Barringtons?"

"Yes," said Jessie with relief. "Do you know where their exhibit is?"

"I remember the name," the man said. "Perhaps because they are brothers. But they are nowhere in this wing, ladies. The Barringtons are in the Scientific Section."

"The Scientific Section?" asked Jessie. "Can you show us where that is?"

The young man pointed out the location on Jessie's map. But as Jessie closed her catalog, he shook his head. "You may want to wait," he added, with a look toward Mrs. Dawson. The older woman had sunk down on a nearby bench and was fanning herself. "It's quite crowded that way right now."

"Why is that?" asked Kat.

"The prince and his party headed there a few moments ago," the man said.

Kat groaned. They were too late to help the brothers!

CHAPTER NINE

Invention Trouble

essie and Kat hurried back to the bench where Mrs. Dawson waited. They quickly explained that they knew where to find the Barringtons.

"But there's a problem," continued Jessie. "The prince is already in the Scientific Section."

"And there's a huge crowd following him," added Kat. "I don't see how we'll ever get to the inventors in time. If they need the part we have, it's too late to help them."

"Nonsense!" said Mrs. Dawson. "We must not give up the battle without a fight, ladies. Follow me." She set off, skirts swaying, back straight, and umbrella firmly in her grip.

Kat knew Mrs. Dawson was right. She and Jessie still needed to get their own bag back—and the time machine.

However, the crowds were every bit as thick as they'd been told. It was hard to make any headway.

"This calls for stronger measures," said Mrs. Dawson. She rolled her eyes and clapped a hand to her forehead. In a voice at once ladylike and loud, she declared, "Dear me! I feel faint."

All around them, people turned to look. A large man moved to Mrs. Dawson's side. "This poor woman has the vapors!" he called. "She must have air!"

"Clear the way!" cried another voice. "Give her room!"

Immediately ahead of them, the crowd parted. And just

beyond, others stepped back to see what was going on. It was as if someone had taken a great knife and cut the crowd in two.

Mrs. Dawson didn't hesitate. With her hand on her forehead and moaning gently, she half led, half dragged Kat. Jessie hurried along behind.

Several people offered to find a place for Mrs. Dawson to sit. But she just sailed on past them.

Suddenly Mrs. Dawson came to a halt. "Oh, my!" she whispered. "That's the prince just ahead."

Kat and Jessie looked. About a dozen men stood in front of them, studying an enormous telescope. At the center of the group was an elegantly dressed, dark-haired man.

"Maybe we're not too late," Kat said. "Unless we've already passed the Barringtons."

"Let's hope we haven't," said Jessie. She looked at Mrs. Dawson, who was fanning herself. The rapid walk, plus the excitement of seeing the prince, had clearly worn her out. "Do you want to rest while we go ahead?" Jessie offered.

"Perhaps that would be a good idea—before I truly *do* have the vapors. I'll just sit on the bench over there," she said.

As Mrs. Dawson found a place to sit, Kat and Jessie edged closer to the royal party. But the prince and his followers were on the move again. Kat and Jessie found themselves caught up in the crowd of reporters and onlookers.

Kat was searching for a way to sneak around the group when a name caught her attention.

"The Barringtons are exhibiting over this way," a short, squarely built man was saying to the prince. "In fact, there's Edward Barrington right now."

Startled, Kat followed the short man's gaze. On the right side of the hall, past the prince, she spotted a familiar figure.

It was the tall, thin man Kat had seen at the station. And he didn't look any happier now than he had then.

"Jessie!" hissed Kat. "There he is!" She pointed out Barrington to her aunt.

"We'll never get to him in time," worried Jessie.

The short man was still talking. "The Barringtons are most eager to have you see their work, your royal majesty."

"And I am looking forward to it as well, Crowley," replied the prince. "I am always interested in those you sponsor."

Crowley began to lead the prince toward Edward Barrington. Kat realized that all she and Jessie could do at this point was follow them.

Suddenly the prince halted. "How fascinating," he commented. "Why, Crowley, this knife has almost 2,000 blades!"

A look of impatience crossed Crowley's face. But he quickly hid it and moved forward to study the knife as well. The crowd behind them did the same.

This was their chance, Kat realized. She led Jessie past the group to the exhibit space where Barrington stood. He was staring at a strange-looking bed and muttering under his breath.

"Mr. Barrington? Mr. Edward Barrington?" Kat asked.

"Yes," replied the man. He turned puzzled eyes to Kat. Then he noticed Jessie—and what she carried.

Jessie handed over the bag. "I believe this is yours, Mr. Barrington. My niece and I picked it up by mistake at the train station. We're truly sorry."

"My word!" Edward Barrington gasped. "Sidney!"

At his shout, a second man popped up from behind the bed. He was as tall and thin as his brother.

"Drat it, Edward!" Sidney cried. "You've made me drop another screw."

"Sidney!" called Edward. "Give that up and come here! We've got our bag back!" As his brother approached, Edward rooted through the bag.

"Here it is!" he said at last. He pulled out the strange device. "Can we get this fastened to the bed in time?"

Sidney glanced down the hall. "I fear not," he answered. "The prince is coming now."

Edward shook his head. "This has only worked correctly once. What if it fails again?" He sighed and straightened his shoulders. "Still, we must make the best of it."

He stuck the bag in a corner, then rushed to the side of the bed. His brother smoothed the few hairs on his head and straightened his jacket. They both stood at attention as Crowley arrived with the prince.

"These are the men I spoke of, your royal highness," Crowley was saying. "Sidney and Edward Barrington. I have been allowing them to use my workshop."

"I am most interested in your idea, gentlemen," Prince Albert said. "From what Mr. Crowley has reported, you are inventors of great promise."

"Thank you, your royal highness," replied Edward, bowing to the prince. Sidney followed suit.

"Now if we could get on with the demonstration," Crowley urged.

Sidney, looking a bit gloomy, lay down on the bed. Then Edward began his explanation. "Our alarm bed is designed to solve a common problem, your royal highness. With it, no one will ever again sleep past the proper waking hour."

Edward moved to the foot of the bed, and Kat inched closer to take a peek. "This is an ordinary alarm clock," Edward said. He pointed to a clock that was attached to the bed frame.

It's just like the clock in the sketch, thought Kat.

"I will set the alarm to go off in 60 seconds," he continued. He did so and stepped back with a nervous smile.

A very long minute passed—and then the bell rang. Edward tensed, while Sidney squeezed his eyes shut.

As for the bed...It just shuddered, hiccuped, and fell still.

From the expression on Prince Albert's face, Kat knew that he was as puzzled as she was.

But Crowley wasn't puzzled—he was angry. His face burned red. And the crowd of onlookers began to murmur. "A waste of time," Kat heard someone whisper.

"We seem to have a problem," Edward said miserably. "I do beg your pardon."

"These things sometimes happen, gentlemen," the prince said kindly. "Please do not let it stop your work."

He moved away from the exhibit, and the crowd followed. All but Crowley. The little man stood in front of the brothers. His cheeks still glowed with anger. And his knuckles were white where they gripped his walking stick.

"You made me look like a fool in front of the prince," he sputtered. "You are finished! Do you understand? Finished!"

Spinning on his heels, Crowley marched out of the exhibit space. His last words floated back over his shoulder. "You will never set foot in my workshop again!"

In the aisles of the exhibit hall, people still talked and laughed. But in the Barringtons' space, there was only silence.

At last Kat found her voice. "I'm so sorry," she said. "This is mostly my fault."

But the Barringtons were—first and last—gentlemen. "Please don't blame yourself, miss," Sidney said.

Edward added, "Indeed. After all, I would have never lost my bag if I hadn't put it on the floor. At least I assume that is what happened?"

Kat nodded. "I think so. Our bag looks just like yours."

At that, Jessie said, "And speaking of our bag, do you have it?"

"You are looking for your bag," stated Edward. If possible, he looked even more unhappy.

"Yes," replied Jessie. "And what was inside it."

"You mean...the machine," said Sidney, suddenly pale.

"That's right," said Kat, wondering what was going on.

"I'm afraid that might be a problem," said Edward.

"Why?" asked Kat and Jessie together.

"Well, we had to find something to replace our missing device," said Edward. "And there was no identification on the bag we had."

Sidney cleared his throat nervously. "Besides, it didn't seem as though the machine in your bag did anything."

Kat and Jessie exchanged a long look. Then Kat moved over to the bed. Getting down on her hands and knees, she peered underneath.

Her eyes followed a metal track along the floor. It curved up to the end of the bed. A length of rope was attached to the track at one end and to the bed at the other.

Kat studied the track more closely. The box-like piece that held the rope to the track looked familiar. The last time Kat had seen it, the chronometer had been sitting inside.

The brothers had taken the time machine apart!

CHAPTER TEN

Faulty Beds & Closed Doors

"Katherine! Whatever are you doing, dear?"

At the sound of Mrs. Dawson's voice, Kat got back to her feet. "I was just looking at the bed," she explained.

"I could see that," Mrs. Dawson responded, staring at Kat's dusty dress. "Though it is hardly ladylike to do so in such a fashion."

Then she turned to the brothers. "I am so pleased to meet you, gentlemen." She shot a meaningful look at Kat and Jessie.

Jessie was the first to realize what Mrs. Dawson's look meant. "Allow me to introduce you." Then she gave a tired smile. "And ourselves as well."

After the introductions were out of the way, Mrs. Dawson continued. "It is most fortunate that the ladies were able to find you. They have been worried about returning your property."

"Well, we didn't return it quite soon enough," said Jessie. She quickly explained the situation to Mrs. Dawson.

When she finished, Edward spoke up. "We are terribly sorry," he said. "But without our spring device, we had to go back to using a rope. And we needed something sturdy to attach it to the bed. So we took your machine apart and used a bit from that."

"Machine?" echoed Mrs. Dawson.

"Yes," said Kat. "We had a machine in our bag. An important one."

"What exactly does—er, did—the machine do?" asked Edward.

"I was still testing it," Jessie replied, avoiding the question. "But now that you have your own device back, we need ours. So if you could give us whatever pieces you used on the bed. And the rest of the machine—"

Jessie broke off when she saw the expressions on the brothers' faces.

"You do have the rest, don't you?" she asked.

"We know where it is," said Sidney.

"But we don't actually *have* it," added Edward. His voice sank lower as he added, "You see, the bag is in Mr. Crowley's workshop."

Kat stared in disbelief. "And he just said he never wanted you to set foot in there again!"

"Surely he'll understand if we tell him what happened," suggested Jessie.

"Mr. Crowley is not known as an understanding person," replied Edward. "Please do not mistake me. We were honored that he was interested in our work. He is a brilliant inventor. And one of the planners of this whole grand exhibition."

Edward glanced at his brother, then he continued. "However, he is...well, a little odd. And very quick-tempered. I fear he will be true to his word and never allow us back into the workshop. Not even to get our bag. He may even throw our things out."

Sidney sighed. "Our careers as inventors are over. And so are our hopes of saving our home."

"But we do feel a duty to make up for your loss, Miss Adams," added Edward. "If you will explain your machine to us, I am sure we can build another. Once we have the materials. And a place to work."

Jessie hesitated. At last she said, "I didn't build the entire machine myself. And I don't have the plans with me. So I'm afraid I can't tell you how to do it."

"Let's at least get one piece back," said Kat to the inventors. "If you can take it off the bed now."

"That's easy enough," said Sidney. He reached under the bed. In a minute, he reappeared with the piece. He handed it to Jessie.

Again it struck Kat how strange the invention was. "Just what is your bed supposed to do?" she asked.

Edward gave his answer with a mix of pride and sadness. "The clock sets things in motion. When the alarm rings, the legs fold, and the bed tips. The sleeper ends up standing on his feet, wide awake."

"Oh," said Kat weakly. *This* was the great invention? A bed that dumped its sleeper off the end? For this the time machine had been sacrificed? For this she and Jessie might be trapped in the past?

But Mrs. Dawson was entranced. "How clever of you," she said. "Why, you simply must get it to work!"

"Maybe I can help," suggested Jessie. Mrs. Dawson looked horrified at the thought of a woman doing such a thing. Even the brothers seemed a bit doubtful.

"She's really handy with machines," said Kat.

"Well, then, if you wouldn't mind taking a look now?" suggested Edward. "I know you are concerned about your own machine. But it would be best to wait a bit before trying the workshop. Mr. Crowley might give us a kinder welcome once he has had a chance to calm down."

That settled it. Everyone gathered around the bed—even Mrs. Dawson.

Sidney explained, "Our problem is having enough force to push the bed upright. And keeping the legs from folding too soon from the weight of the sleeper."

He picked up the device that had been in Edward's bag. "We had hoped this heavy spring might do the job. If we could just get it attached correctly."

Jessie studied the bed, then looked at the piece Sidney held. "May I?" she said, reaching for it.

"Of course," said Sidney.

"Now, gentlemen, if you'll lend me a hand," said Jessie.

As Jessie directed, Sidney held up the end of the bed. Edward knelt beside her, holding the piece in place. Kat stood close by so she could hand screws to her aunt. And Mrs. Dawson watched everything with interest.

After 15 minutes of tinkering, Jessie was satisfied. "There," she declared. "With the spring connected like that, your bed might work."

The brothers stared at her handiwork. "By Jove, this could do it!" cried Edward. "Let's give it a try, shall we?"

The brothers lowered the bed. While Sidney lay down, Edward set the alarm again.

When the alarm went off, the bed shook. The legs jerked backward. But the bed stayed in place—and so did Sidney.

However, neither Barrington was upset. Sidney and Edward quickly compared notes with Jessie.

At last Edward nodded. "Yes, Miss Adams. I think it will work now. It is just a matter of a few minor changes. How ever can we thank you for your help?"

"Simply telling us how to find Mr. Crowley will be thanks enough," said Jessie. "With any luck, he'll be less angry by the time we reach him."

"Well, we don't know where he lives," Edward admitted. "But we can try taking you to his workshop..."

"Just give us the address," suggested Jessie. "We'll go on our own. Surely he won't turn away two American visitors."

"We'll explain what happened," added Kat. "I know he'll give us our bag back after he's heard our story. He might also be willing to give you a second chance."

"I doubt that," Sidney commented. "But here is the address." He quickly wrote it on a slip of paper and gave it to Jessie.

Leaving the brothers to their work, Kat, Jessie, and Mrs. Dawson hurried to the entrance. Outside, Thomas was waiting with the carriage, as promised. Jessie gave him the address, and they were off.

A half-hour ride brought them to a tall brick building. Kat dashed up the walk, with Jessie and Mrs. Dawson following.

But when they reached the door, they found a small sign posted:

The workshop will be closed for the week in honor of the Great Exhibition.

Richard Crowley

"Closed for the week!" exclaimed Jessie.

"So it appears, my dear," sighed Mrs. Dawson. "I am sorry."

"We can't wait a week!" cried Kat. "By then, he may have thrown everything away!"

But no one had a solution to the problem. They had no idea where Crowley lived. In any case, he would probably spend much of his time at the exhibition. And there was little chance they'd be able to spot him there.

The carriage ride back to Mrs. Dawson's house was long and silent. Kat kept thinking, trying to come up with some way to get the bag back. She could tell from Jessie's wrinkled forehead that her aunt was doing the same thing.

But as the carriage pulled to a halt, it was Mrs. Dawson who suggested the next step. "Ladies, I do not wish to raise false hopes," she warned. "But perhaps—just perhaps—I can help you reach Mr. Crowley."

CHAPTER ELEVEN

A Message at the Ball

 ou know how to reach Mr. Crowley?" said Jessie. "That's wonderful!"

"I said perhaps," Mrs. Dawson reminded her. "Follow me."

She led Kat and Jessie to the parlor, where she plucked a card from the mantel. "This is how you may be able to find Mr. Crowley," she declared. She handed the card to Jessie.

"It's an invitation to a ball that's being given tomorrow," noted Jessie. "I'm afraid I don't see how that will help."

"Lady Rutherford is an old friend of mine," said Mrs. Dawson. "She is giving the ball to honor those who organized the exhibition. As you probably noted, I am allowed to bring guests. So I would like you to come with me."

"Do you think Mr. Crowley will attend?" asked Jessie.

"Of course he will. He would never refuse an invitation from Lord and Lady Rutherford, my dear. Not if he wants to maintain his standing in London society."

Jessie nodded. "It's certainly worth a try. Besides, it should be an interesting experience."

"It'll be wonderful, Jessie!" Kat burst in excitedly. "But what will we wear?"

Mrs. Dawson turned astonished eyes on Kat. "Katherine, dear, you seem to have misunderstood me. I will see that your aunt has something to wear. But you cannot go with us. Girls your age do not attend such affairs. Not before they come out. It just is not done."

Kat stared at her in confusion. She asked, " 'Come out'? What do girls come out of?"

Kat could see that Jessie was trying not to laugh. But Mrs. Dawson answered seriously. "Really, I had thought such customs were known even in America!"

She went on to explain that girls from "proper" families "came out" when they reached the age of 17 or 18. They went to parties and balls and were presented in court, where they met the queen. It was all a sign that they were part of London society. And ready for a suitable marriage, she added.

"A very good system," Jessie remarked. "For those who are going to be part of London society. However, Katherine never will be. And attending a ball would be such an educational experience for her, don't you think?"

"Besides," added Kat, "I'm the one who's mostly responsible for what happened to the Barringtons. And Mr. Crowley might have a harder time saying no to me than he would to an adult."

Kat waited anxiously while Mrs. Dawson thought over the suggestion. At last the older woman nodded. "Very well. Given what is at stake, I agree. Katherine will go with us."

She turned to Kat. "But you will be there to make your request, Katherine—nothing else. You cannot participate. And you must be very quiet."

"I'll just look around for Mr. Crowley," Kat promised.

"Now we have much to do before tomorrow evening," Mrs. Dawson said. "We must get you both outfitted. And a few lessons in manners and dance steps might be in order."

They were soon caught up in a whirlwind of preparations. First Mrs. Dawson sent Lucy to the attic. "Some of my daughter Emily's old ball gowns are there," she told Kat and Jessie.

Lucy returned to the room with several lovely dresses. Jessie found that she could fit into Emily's clothing. However, it meant lacing her corset a bit tighter.

Kat was more of a problem. She tried on a beautiful gown with layers of rosy pink and creamy lace. But it dragged on the floor and hung like a sack from her shoulders.

Lucy came up with a solution. "Mum fixes up the clothing you give me so it fits just fine," she told Mrs. Dawson. "We can pin things so the dress fits Kat—I mean, Miss Katherine. Then I'll take it home with me. I know Mum would be happy to sew it up tonight."

"That's a great idea!" exclaimed Kat. "And we can pay her for her work. Can't we, Jessie?"

Mrs. Dawson and Lucy tucked and pinned the dress. And all the while, Mrs. Dawson instructed her visitors about proper behavior. Most of the lecture was for Jessie's benefit, since Kat was forbidden to do anything but watch. For instance, Jessie was told she couldn't dance with the same gentleman more than three times in a row. She should never express her own opinions. On the other hand, she must show great interest in the opinions of her dance partners. The list went on and on.

"There!" announced Mrs. Dawson at last. "That should do it!" Kat wasn't sure if she was referring to the gown—or to their lessons. Probably both.

～

Kat was sure that the time before the ball would drag. But to her amazement, the next day sped by. Perhaps it was because there was so much to do.

Now, with less than an hour before the ball, Kat stood before the mirror. "You look like a proper lady," commented Lucy.

"Thanks to your mother," Kat noted. "She did a wonderful job. The gown fits like it was made for me."

"I'm glad Mrs. Dawson asked me to work late tonight," replied Lucy. "So I could see you all dressed up."

"I wish you were going with me," sighed Kat. "Think how much fun we could have."

"Fun?" laughed Lucy. "At a fancy ball? Can't say that it seems much fun to me having to be all stiff and ladylike. You can't even eat much, for fear of dripping on your gown."

The two girls were giggling at the thought when Jessie entered the room. "I overheard that," she said. "And I have to agree with Lucy. I can't imagine how I'll ever manage to dance in this. Let alone eat."

Kat spun around to look at her aunt. "Oh, Jessie!" Kat breathed. Jessie's hair was swept up on top of her head. In her white gloves and wide satin skirts, she looked elegant—and beautiful.

Mrs. Dawson hurried in to join them. She too looked quite handsome in her lacy ivory dress. "It is time, ladies," she said.

With Lucy watching from the door, the three ball-goers made their way to the carriage. Even Kat needed help from Thomas this time. She was finding that a wide, trailing skirt wasn't the easiest thing to move about in.

Before long they arrived at the Rutherfords. The huge house, set back on a velvety lawn, glowed with dozens of lights. Through the windows, Kat caught glimpses of beautifully dressed people.

They were greeted at the entrance by Lady Rutherford and her two daughters. Lady Rutherford gave a surprised glance Kat's way. But she nodded in understanding when Mrs. Dawson introduced her as "a young guest from America."

One of the daughters handed Jessie a card that listed the evening's dances. Kat knew that gentlemen were expected to sign up for the pleasure of dancing with a lady.

Jessie and Kat followed Mrs. Dawson farther into the house. Kat peeked into each room as they passed by. In one, food and drinks were being served. In another, people sat at tables and played cards.

They continued on toward the back of the house. Mrs. Dawson pointed out a room filled with men, most of whom were smoking. "That room is for gentlemen only," she warned. "No lady would set foot in there."

At last they reached a huge set of double doors. These stood open, revealing an enormous ballroom. The ceiling soared overhead, and the polished marble floor gleamed in the candlelight. In a far corner, hidden behind potted plants, several musicians were tuning their instruments.

The ballroom was filled with men and women dressed in their finest. They stood in small groups, carrying on quiet conversations.

"The dancing is about to begin. So I will leave the two of you here," Mrs. Dawson said. "Do enjoy yourself, Miss Adams. And Katherine, remember that you are only here to watch for Mr. Crowley."

"But where are you going?" asked Kat.

"My dancing days are long over, my dear. If you need me, you will find me playing cards." With that, she headed back

the way they'd come.

"Do you see Mr. Crowley anywhere?" asked Kat.

"No," sighed Jessie. "And if he spends his evening in the 'gentlemen only' room, we may never spot him."

They hadn't been there long when a young man approached Jessie. He bowed and introduced himself. "Is your dance card filled, Miss Adams?" he asked.

Jessie handed over the card, and the young man signed up for the first dance. He was followed by another gentleman. And another. Soon Jessie's entire dance card was filled. And when the music began, she was swept onto the marble floor.

Kat watched as her aunt danced, her long skirts swirling about her feet. Mrs. Dawson's lessons seemed to have done the trick. Jessie looked as though she'd been attending fancy balls for years.

Well, it seems as if Jessie is going to be pretty busy, Kat thought. I may as well start looking for Mr. Crowley.

She made her way out of the ballroom and began to explore. She checked in every room—except the one Mrs. Dawson had warned her about. But there was no sign of Crowley anywhere.

Kat was about to give up when she noticed a group of men enter the hall. Crowley was with them!

For a time, the men just stood there, talking. Then Crowley began to head for the front of the house. The others followed.

Can they be leaving already? Kat wondered.

She decided that she couldn't wait for Jessie. She'd have to speak to Crowley herself. Gathering up her skirts, Kat hurried after him.

As she drew closer, she overheard one of the other men. "I do wish you would stay a while longer, sir. I am most interested in your ideas about electricity."

"I am sorry, Smithers," said Crowley. "You will have to make an appointment to speak to me later. I must make a short evening of it. I have an early meeting tomorrow at the exhibition."

It's now or never, Kat realized. She stepped around the others to stand in front of Crowley. "Good evening, Mr. Crowley," she said, dropping a curtsy. "Please, sir, could I talk to you for just a moment?"

Crowley's eyes widened. "Whatever are you doing here, child? You're not Lord Rutherford's youngest daughter, are you? Why, you sound...American." He said the last word as if it were a disease.

Kat looked the little man in the eye. Politely, she replied, "Yes, sir. I am American. I came to London to visit your wonderful exhibition."

"I see," said Crowley, turning to leave. "Well, you shall just have to get your ticket at the entrance. I have none to give out."

"It's not that, sir," Kat quickly protested. "I've been to the exhibition already." She took a deep breath and went on. "You see, Mr. Crowley, you have a bag that belongs to me. And I need it back right away."

"Don't be ridiculous!" snapped Crowley. "I have never seen you before. How could I have something that belongs to you?"

"Well, there was a mix-up. The Barrington brothers ended up with—"

Crowley interrupted with a snort. "The Barrington brothers! Let me assure you, I do not want to talk about them."

"But Mr. Crowley," Kat said. "It wasn't their fault the

invention didn't work. Please let me tell you what happened. Maybe then you'll understand about the bag. And maybe you'll be willing to give them a second chance."

"There are no second chances, my dear," said Crowley. "Not when I have been made to look a fool." To a passing servant, he said, "My evening cloak, please."

As the servant rushed off, Kat made one last try. "Please, sir. If you'd just let me explain."

"Explain what, child?" someone asked quietly. "Why are you so upset?"

At the sound of that familiar voice, everyone turned— even Crowley.

CHAPTER TWELVE

A Second Chance

Your royal highness!" someone exclaimed. Everyone in the crowd bowed.

Kat curtsied to the figure in the doorway. She was too stunned to speak.

Prince Albert moved forward. Again he asked, "What did you want to explain, child? I'm sure Mr. Crowley wants to hear. As do I."

"I—I—I was telling Mr. Crowley about how my bag got mixed up with the Barringtons' bag," stammered Kat. "You see, that's why their invention didn't work, your majesty," she added. "It was my fault. Mine and my aunt's."

"Ah, the alarm bed," said the prince. "A clever idea. I was sorry it failed to work. Please do explain."

So Kat told her story again. "Now the Barringtons have the part they need," she concluded. "And I'm sure they can get the bed to work. If only you could see it again."

"Your concern for the Barringtons is touching, my dear," said the prince. "As is your desire to correct your mistake."

He turned to Crowley. "We will both be at the exhibition again tomorrow. We must pay the brothers another visit."

"Of course, your royal highness," croaked Mr. Crowley.

With that, the prince nodded and headed down the hall. The group of men who had surrounded Crowley now moved along behind the prince. Soon Kat and the little man were the only ones left.

"Mr. Crowley, about my bag," began Kat.

But Crowley cut her off. "Tell the Barringtons they had better be sure that bed works tomorrow," he spat out. He turned and marched toward the front door.

Kat sighed unhappily. There was nothing more she could do now except report back to Jessie. And hope that the brothers' invention really was in working order. Maybe then Crowley would listen to her about the bag. Otherwise, she and Jessie might never be able to return to their own time.

~

"You must eat a bit more, Miss Adams," fussed Mrs. Dawson. "After all, you are going to see the prince later this morning. It would never do to faint from hunger."

"The prince," sighed Lucy as she put a pot of jam on the breakfast table. Eyes shining, she looked at Kat. "I can't believe you actually talked to him."

"Neither can I," laughed Kat. "But he was so kind!"

"I'd give anything to see him up close," said Lucy. "Even though I'd never dare speak to him."

Lucy hurried off and the others finished eating. "We'd better get going," said Jessie. "We need to warn the Barringtons about their visitors."

"I will send Lucy to tell Thomas you are ready," said Mrs. Dawson.

"Aren't you going to go with us?" asked Kat.

"Not this time," answered Mrs. Dawson. "I find myself very tired after last night's event."

A thought struck Kat. At first she wasn't sure she should even mention it. Then she decided she had to.

"Mrs. Dawson," she began. "If you aren't going, well..."

"Well what, Katherine?" said Mrs. Dawson. "Speak your mind, my dear."

"I was just thinking that there would be room in the carriage for another person. And..." She finished in a rush of words. "And Lucy would really like to go. It would be such a good experience for her. And I could help her catch up with her work later. And..."

She fell silent as she noted Mrs. Dawson's surprised look. "Lucy?" the older woman repeated.

"Yes, ma'am," replied Kat as she glanced at her aunt.

Jessie seconded her. "It does seem like a good idea. That is, if you can spare Lucy for a few hours, Mrs. Dawson. As you noted yourself, this is a chance to see the finest accomplishments of England. And of the world."

Mrs. Dawson was quiet for a moment. Then she said, "Why...Well, why not? It would be good for the child."

So a very excited Lucy soon found herself with Kat and Jessie inside the Crystal Palace. They went straight to the Barringtons' exhibit. There they found the brothers still tinkering with their invention. After introducing her friend, Kat circled the bed. "Does it work?" she asked eagerly.

"More often than not," replied Edward with satisfaction. "Though this spring isn't quite as strong as it should be."

"Maybe you should demonstrate it with someone lighter on it," suggested Jessie. "You want to be certain it works today." She went on to explain what had happened at the ball.

"The prince is returning?" asked Sidney in disbelief.

"We must have another trial first!" exclaimed Edward.

"With someone lighter, as you said."

But it was too late. A buzz of voices nearby told them that the prince and his party were on the way.

As they came closer, Lucy gasped. "Oh, heavens! It's the queen herself!" she cried.

Kat stared in wonder at the figure who held Prince Albert's arm. The short, plump woman was familiar from her history books. Yet there was a grace to her movements that no picture showed. Victoria was every inch the queen.

The party reached the Barringtons. Nervously, the two brothers bowed to the queen and her husband. And then it was time to begin.

"Welcome, your majesties," Edward said. "My brother and I are pleased to demonstrate the amazing alarm bed."

With the new plan in mind, Sidney turned toward Kat. He's going ask me to help! she thought.

But just then, Kat caught sight of Lucy's wide-eyed look. So as Sidney approached, Kat gave Lucy a tiny push forward.

Sidney took the hint. "Perhaps Miss Lucy might help us," he suggested.

Eyes dancing, Lucy took her place on the bed. Edward bent down to set the alarm.

The seconds ticked off loudly in the hushed silence. Then the alarm rang. As smoothly as if it had always worked, the legs folded, and the bed tilted up. Lucy was left standing on her feet. With a blush, she curtsied to the crowd.

A broad smile spread over the queen's face. "We are most amused," she announced regally.

The prince looked at his wife fondly. "I thought you might be," he said.

Seeing the royal reaction, others in the group began to

clap. A large red-haired woman at the edge of the crowd came forward.

"I must have one of these!" she declared.

"And I," added another voice.

Taking Prince Albert's outstretched hand, the queen graced the inventors with a smile. Then she and her husband continued down the hall.

But this time, a number of people remained behind. Some talked to the brothers about ordering beds. One, a reporter, was asking Lucy how it felt to use the alarm bed.

Crowley stayed as well, taking in the scene. The red-haired woman approached him. "Well done, Crowley," she said. "You do seem to find the cleverest inventors."

"Thank you, Lady Hardwick," said Mr. Crowley, stroking his mustache. "I like to think I have a sharp eye for talent."

As the woman moved away, Jessie caught Kat's eye. She nodded toward Crowley. Then she and Kat closed in on the little man.

"Mr. Crowley," said Jessie. "If we might have a word with you?"

Crowley tore his eyes away from the alarm bed and its admirers. "Yes?" he said.

This time he listened to Kat's story. And he agreed that, of course, they should come right to his workshop. "If only you ladies had come to me with your problem earlier," he purred.

It was past noon by the time they left the workshop. Mr. Crowley had insisted on showing them around. He made a point of telling them exactly where the Barrington brothers would be working.

At last they were in the carriage, headed back to Mrs. Dawson's house. Jessie held the black bag's handle tightly. Even so, Kat never took her eyes off the piece of luggage. She wasn't taking any chances with losing it again.

At the house, the three had to share the entire experience with Mrs. Dawson. The older woman's eyes kept going to Lucy. The girl offered comments only when asked. Still, it was clear that she could barely contain her excitement.

When they wrapped up their tale, Jessie asked that she and Kat be excused. "We'd like to check on the contents of our bag," she explained. "To see if we can put the machine back together."

"And I'd best be getting to my work," said Lucy. She looked at Mrs. Dawson. "I already thanked Miss Adams for taking me. But I want to thank you too, ma'am. It was good of you to give me the time."

As Lucy turned to leave the room, Mrs. Dawson called to her. "Wait, Lucy. There is no need to dust today."

Lucy gazed at her employer in surprise. "Ma'am?"

"The dust will wait until tomorrow," said Mrs. Dawson firmly. "Right now, I want you to choose something to read to me. I would truly enjoy that."

Lucy's eyes shone. "I'd enjoy it too, ma'am," she said.

"Very well," replied Mrs. Dawson. "Off with you, then. Find a suitable book."

Lucy darted out of the room, her face lit with joy.

With a smile, Kat followed Jessie upstairs to their own room. There they dumped the contents of the bag onto the rug. Kat added the piece they had gotten from the brothers.

Together they stared at the jumbled parts. The time

machine hadn't been completely taken apart. The legs, which Jessie had unfolded, were still attached to the body of the device. But almost everything else had been unscrewed, unlatched, and undone.

Jessie sat back with a groan. "Oh, Kat. I'm not sure we'll ever be able to put it together again."

CHAPTER THIRTEEN

No Time Like the Present

he time machine *was* a mess. But it was their only way home, so Jessie got to work.

Kat helped by handing her parts and holding things steady. A couple of times, Jessie had to back up and try things another way. Finally the last piece was in place.

"It looks the same," said Kat hopefully.

"On the outside," commented Jessie. "I guess we won't know if everything's the same inside until we try it."

Kat sighed. "It will be good to get home," she said. "But I'm going to miss Lucy. I think I'm even going to miss Mrs. Dawson a little!"

"I know what you mean," said Jessie. "It's been quite an adventure. Now if we can just end it safely..."

She reached for the traveling bag. "Let's get packed," she suggested. "Then we can tell everyone we're leaving."

"How are we going to do this, Jessie?" asked Kat. "We can't just disappear from Mrs. Dawson's house in a puff of smoke!"

"We'll tell her we're taking the train," said Jessie. "We can set up the time machine somewhere near the station."

Kat nodded. She found the encyclopedia where she'd tucked it under the bed. That went into the bag along with the folded-up time machine.

"Can we take this back with us?" she asked. She was holding her ticket stub from the exhibition.

"We can try," said Jessie.

So Kat dropped it into her purse. Then they headed downstairs.

They found Mrs. Dawson in the parlor. Lucy was gone, but a book lay open on the table nearby.

"We've come to say good-bye, Mrs. Dawson," said Jessie. "And to thank you for being so kind."

"Must you leave already?" asked Mrs. Dawson as she got to her feet.

"Yes," replied Jessie. "We have a long way to travel."

"I will miss your company," said Mrs. Dawson. "As will Lucy, I am sure."

At that Kat asked, "May I go and say good-bye to her?"

"Of course. She's in the kitchen accepting a delivery. You can ask her to have Thomas bring the carriage around to the front. He'll take you to the station."

Jessie started to protest. But Mrs. Dawson held up a hand. "Please. I insist. And Katherine," she added, "have Lucy return to the parlor with you. I know she will want to say farewell to Miss Adams as well."

Kat dashed back to the kitchen to find her friend. "Lucy, I've come to say good-bye," she said.

"Good-bye?" Lucy echoed. "Oh, Kat! I knew you'd have to leave. I just wish it didn't have to be so soon."

"I know," said Kat. "I really want to go home. But I do wish I had more time to spend here."

The two girls headed for the carriage house to get Thomas. Then they walked back, still talking.

"How did the reading go?" asked Kat.

"It was wonderful!" cried Lucy. "And you're never going to believe what Mrs. Dawson has planned! She's going to teach me in the afternoons! She says she's got a grand book of maps up in the attic. And she's going to show me how to do sums and things. She even says the dust can pile up, as long as I get to the market and do the cooking. I can't believe it!"

"That's fantastic, Lucy!" said Kat.

Together they headed for the parlor. Jessie had just finished paying Mrs. Dawson for use of the room. Now she pulled one more thing out of the traveling bag.

"Kat and I would like you to have this," she said. She handed a slip of paper to Mrs. Dawson.

"Why, this is a week's pass to the exhibition!" exclaimed Mrs. Dawson.

"Yes," said Jessie. "Mr. Crowley gave it to us when we visited his workshop. Kat and I can't use it, so we'd like you to have it."

"My goodness," said the older woman. "A whole week of visits! And good for two people," she noted.

She looked over at Lucy, whose eyes were wide with hope. "Would you like to go with me, Lucy?" she asked. "It would mean working a bit later every day to get your chores done."

"Oh yes, ma'am," said Lucy in a rush. "I wouldn't mind how hard I had to work. Truly I wouldn't."

"Very well," said Mrs. Dawson. "We shall go this afternoon. As soon as Thomas returns with the carriage."

It was time to say their farewells. Kat hugged Lucy. And Lucy hugged her back. Then with a final wave, Kat and Jessie set off in the carriage.

Just before the bridge over the Thames River, Jessie called Thomas to a halt. "We'll get out here."

"But, miss, the train station's on the other side of the river."

"I know," said Jessie. "Kat and I would like to walk the rest of the way. It's such a fine day. And it will be our last view of London."

"I understand, miss," said Thomas. He pulled over and helped them from the carriage. Then with a tip of his hat and his best wishes, he was gone.

Jessie gazed down the bank. "We need a hidden spot to set up the time machine," she said.

"How about over there?" asked Kat. She pointed to a small grove of bushy trees.

"Perfect."

In a matter of moments, they were hidden from sight. Jessie set up the machine and stepped back. "Well, here goes," she said. "I don't know what we're going to do if it doesn't work."

She and Kat took off their medallions and placed them in the drawer of the machine.

"Hooray!" shouted Kat when the machine began to hum. But that's all it did.

Jessie frowned. "I guess I didn't put it together correctly."

"Wait a minute. If it's humming, it must be working," Kat insisted. "Let's just think of what should happen next."

They thought back to their first trip. The medallions had been in place, just as they were now. They had both been holding on to a handle of the machine. Had they done anything else?

"I've got it!" declared Kat. "It's not what *we* do. It's what the sun does! We didn't go anywhere until the sun hit the medallions! I'm sure that's it."

"I think you're right," said Jessie. She looked up at the leafy roof over their heads. "We're going to have to move out of here."

They checked to see that no one was close by. Then they carried the machine out of the grove of trees.

At once sunlight poured over the time machine. Suddenly the medallions began to glow. And a cloud of mist rose up. Kat and Jessie closed their eyes and held on tightly.

Next thing they knew, the sound of excited barking filled the air.

It was Newton! Kat opened her eyes. They were home! Back in the lab, back in their normal clothes.

Kat almost sobbed in relief. She let go of the time machine and dropped to her knees. "Newton!" she cried, throwing her arms around the dog. "I'm so glad to see you!"

"That makes two of us," Jessie added with a shaky smile. "Oh, Kat, it worked! We made it back!"

"Was there ever any doubt?" asked Kat. She began to laugh, and Jessie joined in.

Jessie's laugh suddenly ended in a gasp. "Kat!" she exclaimed.

"What is it?" Kat asked, jumping to her feet.

"Look at the clock!"

"Twelve o'clock," observed Kat. "So?"

"Just before you managed to start the machine up, I had checked the time," said Jessie slowly. "It was almost noon. I remember because I was thinking about fixing lunch."

"So we're back at the same time of day as when we left," said Kat.

"I wonder if that's all," murmured Jessie. She reached over and flipped on the radio she kept in the lab.

Music filled the room. When the song ended, the announcer broke in. "Now the news for August fourth. Today in Washington—"

Jessie turned off the radio. "August fourth," she said softly.

"The same day we left," Kat added.

Jessie began to pace back and forth. "This is fascinating! Almost no time passed. So no one could have known we were gone. And nothing could have happened while we were away. Maybe the chronometer really worked after all. It was just measuring time here—in the present."

"That means there's nothing to stop us from going whenever we want," said Kat. "That's great, Jessie! When can we take our next trip?"

"Whoa there, kiddo," replied her aunt. "Not so fast. Who says there will be another trip? And even if there is, I'm not sure you'll be going."

"Jessie! You can't do that!" Kat protested. "I'm your assistant. I'm the one who helped you get the time machine going."

Jessie studied her niece's excited face. Then she sighed. "We'll talk about that later. Right now I want to get things put away." She reached for the traveling bag.

"Well, the bag looks like it did before the trip," Jessie commented as she unzipped it. "And the encyclopedia is still here."

"That reminds me," said Kat. "The purse I had in London

is gone. I wonder if the things I had in there are back in my pockets."

She patted the pockets of her jeans. Something was there! Kat eagerly removed the contents. Her folding hairbrush had returned to its original form. And once again, she had a few wrinkled tissues.

"My money is gone," she commented. "I guess that makes sense, since we spent the money we arrived with."

But there was still something else. Kat pulled out a small rectangle of paper, yellowed with age and crumbling at the edges.

"Look, Jessie! It's my ticket stub from the exhibition," she said softly. "But now it looks like an antique."

"It is," said Jessie. "At least in our time."

Kat placed the ticket gently on the worktable. Then she turned back to her aunt. "I have to know, Jessie. Are we going to make another trip?"

Jessie laughed. "You won't rest until you have an answer, will you?"

"How could I?"

"All right, Kat. I'll make you a promise. If I go again, you can too."

"Great!" exclaimed Kat, throwing her arms around Jessie. She knew that her aunt would never be able to resist trying the machine again.

Kat's mind danced with thoughts of their next journey. It didn't matter where—or when—they went. She was ready for another adventure in the past.

More to Explore

Have fun exploring more about life in London during the time of the Great Exhibition. And there are great projects for you to do too!

The Story Behind the Story

In spring of 1851, London was packed with visitors. They came from every corner of the globe to attend the Exhibition of the Works of Industry of All Nations.

The Great Exhibition was a project dear to the heart of Prince Albert. For that reason, it was also important to his loving wife, Queen Victoria. Albert worked long and hard to make the exhibition a success. He saw it as an attempt to bring peace to the nations of the world.

At first the prince's project was met with much protest. Some hated the idea of "ruining" the beauty of Hyde Park by putting a building there. Others were afraid that the huge number of visitors from other countries would bring dirt and disease with them. And some just disliked the idea of having so many foreigners in the heart of England.

Despite all these roadblocks, the Great Exhibition opened on May 1. By the time it closed in October, over six million visitors had come to see the 100,000 exhibits.

Exhibitors from more than 40 nations took part in the show. But the majority of the displays were from England and its colonies. In fact, the exhibition revealed a lot about life in Victorian England. As Queen Victoria remarked, "It goes to prove that we are capable of doing almost anything."

Certainly this was true in the area of mechanical products. By this time, the Industrial Revolution had taken hold. Every kind of machine—from cannons to telegraphs to printers—filled the Crystal Palace.

Also on view were items that to modern minds might seem odd and even a bit silly. There really were displays of small animals, stuffed and arranged into scenes. And there really was an alarm bed that dumped the sleeper into a standing position. (Though the Barringtons weren't actually the inventors.) The bed was offered with a basin of cold water—in case being thrown onto your feet wasn't enough to wake you!

"Marvelous," "ugly," and "ridiculous." All three words

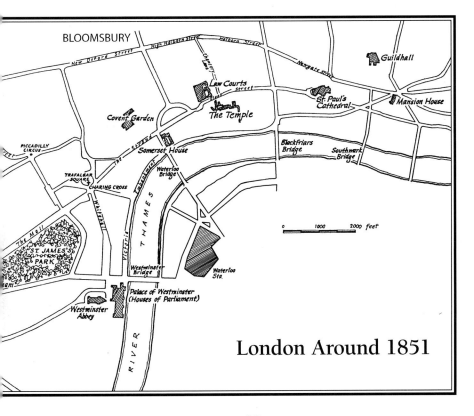

London Around 1851

can be applied to the exhibition and to Victorian life itself. During Queen Victoria's rule (1837–1901), life ran according to strict rules. Those rules helped some English people achieve greatness. However, the same rules held many back—especially women.

Despite the fact that a woman ruled the country, women and girls were limited in their choices. As a ten-year-old, Kat would never have been allowed to go to a ball—or to do anything else very exciting. She probably wouldn't have attended school either. Boys from wealthy families were often sent away to be educated. But education wasn't considered necessary for girls—not even girls from well-to-do families.

As Kat saw during her visit to Lucy's home, there was a great gap between the rich and poor at this time. There were numerous people with great wealth. And there was a large, growing middle class—of which Mrs. Dawson would have been a part. But the streets of London were also filled with the poor and homeless. Many of them were much worse off than Lucy.

Life was especially hard for the children of the poor. During the middle of the century, nearly ten percent of working-class children were orphaned before they reached the age of 15. The free ragged schools Lucy talks of did exist. However, most of those who attended were boys—and most of them only managed to spend a few hours a week in school.

At the time of Victoria's death (1901), change was coming to English society. Many of the strict rules of behavior were no longer observed. And the divisions between rich and poor had gradually lessened.

The fate of the Crystal Palace reflected the changing times. In 1852 the structure was taken down, moved, and reassembled. It continued to attract visitors until it was destroyed by fire in 1936. Still, its memory calls to mind both the best and the worst of the Victorian age.

Victorian Manners

In Queen Victoria's time, much attention was paid to good manners. There were rules of correct behavior for almost every situation.

The lists below give just a few of the rules of Victorian behavior. After you've finished reading, study the picture on the next page. Can you spot some of the rules that are being broken?

A lady...

- never spends time alone with a man unless she's married or over the age of 30.
- never walks alone except to church or a park.
- never calls on a gentleman alone, unless for business purposes.
- never wears pearls or diamonds in the morning.
- never dances more than three dances with the same partner.
- never stands with her hands on her hips.
- never sits with her legs crossed.
- always sits up straight with a graceful posture.

A gentleman...

- always walks ahead of a lady when going up stairs.
- always sits facing backward when riding in a carriage with a lady.
- gets out of the carriage first so he can help the lady down.
- never smokes when ladies are present.
- never leans against things while standing or sitting.

- never wears his hat inside.

- never puts his feet on the furniture.

- doesn't cross his legs when seated or standing.

- always tips his hat to a lady when he meets her outside—but not until after she first bows to him.

- never speaks to a lady he doesn't know well unless she speaks first.

Answers: Lady #1 has her hands on her hips. Lady #2 isn't sitting up straight. Gentleman #3 is wearing his hat inside. (And he shouldn't sit on the chair backward either!) Gentleman #4 is leaning against the wall and standing with his legs crossed. Gentleman #5 has his foot on the furniture. Gentleman #6 is smoking in front of the ladies and leaning his head against the wall.

Teatime

Tea holds a special place in the hearts of the British. It was introduced into Britain in the 1600s and is still popular today.

The British drink tea almost any time of the day. But it is afternoon tea—a tradition that developed in the 1800s—that has become most famous. Usually it takes place around 4:00 or 5:00. For some people, teatime bridges the gap between lunch and a late dinner. That means that more than just tea is served. Bread (or toast) and butter, small sandwiches, biscuit-like scones, pastries, and cakes might also be offered.

Celebrate this tradition by inviting guests to tea. Use the ideas on these pages to plan your party.

A Hot Item

Tea was a popular beverage in eighteenth-century England. It was also very expensive. Those who could afford tea leaves kept them under lock and key. Some dishonest merchants saw this as an opportunity. They bought used tea leaves from servants, then dried and resold them. Other merchants went even further, selling dyed tree leaves as tea!

Making the tea

Ask an adult to help you make tea the proper British way. Heat cold water in a teakettle until it comes to a boil. Pour a little of the hot water into a teapot to warm the pot. Then pour that out. Add a tea bag* for each person who will be having tea. Then carefully fill the pot with hot water. Let the tea sit for a few minutes to *steep*, or brew. Serve in china cups. Offer your guests milk, lemon, and sugar to flavor their tea.

Dressing for Tea

By the 1870s, teatime was an important part of the day for England's well-to-do. Rich ladies even changed out of their day dresses into gowns made just for afternoon tea. (Naturally, these were called "tea gowns.") Then they might change again for dinner. So a woman might wear three or more lovely dresses in a single day.

*If you want to be really British, use loose tea leaves in a tea strainer. You will need one teaspoonful of tea leaves for each cup of tea.

Teatime treats

Besides tea, you'll want to serve snacks. You can make or buy small cupcakes, muffins, sweet breads, or biscuits. You could also make tea sandwiches by following the directions below.

Tea Sandwiches

Cut the crusts off some thinly sliced bread. Butter one side of the bread. Then add one of the following fillings:
- jam or jelly
- finely chopped hard-boiled egg mixed with a little mayonnaise, salt, and pepper
- thinly sliced cucumbers

Place a second slice of bread on top of the filling. Cut each sandwich into small squares or triangles.

Setting the table

Arrange everything on your tea table. Put a pretty cloth over the table, or use place mats. Then set places for yourself and your guests. You will each need a small plate, a teacup and saucer, and a teaspoon. Add napkins and napkin rings too. If you don't have napkin rings, you can make them from wide ribbon or a decorated paper band.

Place a bouquet of real or artificial flowers at the center of the tea table. Or make individual nosegays for each guest by tying a ribbon around the stems of a small bunch of flowers.

Arrange your teatime treats on a platter or small tray. You may want to put a fancy paper doily underneath the food. Put the teapot on the table too. Then settle back (in a graceful posture, of course) and enjoy a relaxing tea.

Stardust Story Sampler

Stardust Classics books feature other heroines to believe in. Come explore with Laurel the Woodfairy and Alissa, Princess of Arcadia. Here are short selections from their books.

Selection from

LAUREL THE WOODFAIRY

"It's no use!" cried Laurel. "I just can't play this tune!"

Laurel lowered her flute. Her beautiful fairy wings drooped as she thought about the long hours she'd spent practicing.

"I'll never be ready for the Celebration of the Chronicles. All the other woodfairies will have some wonderful poem or picture or dance to share. But I won't have a thing."

Her contribution to the Celebration had to be just right. It should capture the beauty and peace of the woods.

"Please let my tune do honor to the Celebration," Laurel whispered. She left the clearing and headed for home.

Laurel had chosen to build her house high in the branches of a huge oak. Most fairies liked to live near the ground. But Laurel loved being close to the breeze, birds, and sunbeams.

Laurel's heart lifted as she entered her cheerful home. She placed her bag on a shelf, then picked up her journal. "Maybe I'll take my journal down to the waterfall," she said softly.

She put her cloak back on and glided to the ground. After settling on a rock near the pond, she began to write.

A sudden movement at the edge of the pond caught Laurel's attention. A tiny head poked through the long grass.

It was her friend Mistletoe the mouse.

Laurel got down off the rock and stretched out on the grass. She propped her chin on her hands so that she was face-to-face with Mistletoe. "Hello!" she said. "What have you been up to lately?"

Mistletoe wiggled her nose. "I went exploring all the way to the edge of the Dappled Woods."

"How exciting!" said Laurel. Like all other fairies, Laurel had never been outside the Dappled Woods.

Mistletoe nervously scratched her ear. "I don't know," she said. "Something seemed wrong."

As Mistletoe spoke, Chitters the chipmunk joined them. Chitters was another of Laurel's animal friends. Now he twitched his furry tail and asked what was going on.

"Mistletoe is worried that something's wrong in the Great Forest," Laurel reported.

Chitters flicked his ears. "Worry, worry. No point in it, I say."

"Mistletoe doesn't worry without a good reason," began Laurel. But she was interrupted by the mouse.

"Listen!" Mistletoe squeaked.

Then they heard it. An unfamiliar noise in the bushes behind them.

Mistletoe sniffed the air wildly. "A stranger!" she exclaimed. "Hide!"

At once the two animals disappeared into the brush.

"A stranger?" Laurel questioned. "But—"

Before she could say another word, someone bumped hard against her. Whoever-it-was tumbled to the ground with a thud.

Laurel jumped to her feet. Someone had tripped over her!

She'd never heard of a fairy who tripped over other fairies before! Except maybe for herself.

Then she noticed something very odd about the other fairy's back. She had no wings! This wasn't a fairy at all!

Selection from

ALISSA, PRINCESS OF ARCADIA

"Good evening."

Princess Alissa jumped off the bench and spun around. Behind her stood an old man cloaked in a glittering robe.

"Who are you?" she asked. "And why are you here? Don't you know that these are the king's private gardens?"

"So they are," said the old man. "And where better to find a princess? For it's you I've come to talk to."

"To me?" said Alissa. "I don't mean to be rude, good sir. But why should I talk to you?"

"Perhaps for the same reason that you want to go on a quest," replied the stranger.

Alissa was startled. How did he know she'd been thinking about a quest?

She stared at the old man in wonder. In the moonlight she could see the long white beard that flowed almost to his waist. And she noticed how his cloak puffed and billowed, though there was no wind.

He continued. "Yes, Alissa, I know a good many things about you. For instance, I know you worry about your new responsibilities. And I think..."

Here he leaned closer and peered nearsightedly. "Just as I thought. You are searching for something."

"But how do you know all this about me?" Alissa asked. "I've never seen you before."

The old man closed his eyes for a moment. "Perhaps you have never seen me. But that doesn't mean I've never seen you."

He opened his eyes. "We will meet again, princess," he said.

"When? And how?" cried Alissa. Suddenly she realized that she wanted to see—had to see—this strange old man again. "And who are you? Where will I find you?"

"Ah," murmured the old man as he combed his fingers through his beard. "All good questions, Alissa. And perhaps a search for the answers should be your first quest."

"My first quest!" exclaimed Alissa. "Am I really to have a quest?"

"We shall see," said the old man. "We shall see. It all depends on you. But you'll need some help. So let this be your guide."

The old man drew himself up. He looked taller and younger—and much more powerful. In ringing tones, he said:

> Unwind this riddle to its end
> If you will seek this strange old man:
> Find me where today becomes tomorrow,
> Yet yesterdays still linger;
> Where neither ground nor air is master.
> In a shelter cloaked in danger.

As soon as he finished speaking, the old man turned to go. Alissa jumped up to follow. She cried out, "Wait! Please wait! What's that supposed to mean?"

But as she started forward, Alissa slipped on the wet ground. By the time she righted herself, all she could see was a swirl of mist. The old man had disappeared into the dark shadows.

"How could he have moved so quickly?" she asked. "Who is he? And what exactly does his riddle mean?" But she received no answers from the empty garden.

STARDUST CLASSICS titles are written under pseudonyms. Authors work closely with Margaret Hall, executive editor of Just Pretend.

Ms. Hall has devoted her professional career to working with and for children. She has a B.S. and an M.S. in education from the State University of New York at Geneseo. For many years, she taught as a classroom and remedial reading teacher for students from preschool through upper elementary. Ms. Hall has also served as an editor with an educational publisher and as a consultant for the Iowa State Department of Education. She has a long history as a freelance writer for the school market, authoring several children's books as well as numerous teacher resources.

KAZUHIKO SANO was born in Tokyo, Japan. He came to the United States to study at the Academy of Art College in San Francisco. After graduation he stayed in the United States and worked as a freelance illustrator. At the same time, he continued his art education, eventually earning a Master of Fine Arts degree.

Mr. Sano works full-time as an illustrator. His art was featured on a movie poster for *The Return of the Jedi* and on promotional materials for the Star Wars trilogy. He has also done paintings of dinosaurs for *Scientific American* magazine and designed a series of United States postal stamps.

Kazuhiko Sano is married and has two young children. He and his family live in Mill Valley, California.

This Book Is Just the Beginning…

Order the new Just Pretend catalog to discover an entire fantasy world beyond the Stardust Classic stories. The Stardust collection includes beautiful dolls with gorgeous clothing, fairytale furniture, and accessories galore. You can set the stage for any adventure imaginable starring your favorite Stardust Classics characters.

There's More to the Just Pretend Story...

The Stardust Classics collection is only one of Just Pretend's many creations for make-believe fun. Our catalog features a variety of playthings for girls and boys ages 2-12. Choose from mix-and-match dress-up sets, costume accessories, over-sized wooden vehicles, role-playing kits, theatrical props—and more!

To request your free Just Pretend catalog, fill out the attached postcard and mail it today. Or call our toll-free number: **1-800-286-7166.**

Just Pretend

Send me a Just Pretend catalog right away.

My name is _____

My address is _____

City_____ State _____ Zip _____

Parent's signature _____

J8BK0001

And send a catalog to my friend too.

My friend's name is _____

My friend's address is _____

City_____ State _____ Zip _____

J8BF0001

Stardust
C L A S S I C S™

If the postcard is missing, you can still get a Just Pretend catalog, featuring the Stardust Classics books and dolls. Send your name and address to:

Just Pretend, Inc.
Stardust Classics
104 Challenger Drive
Portland, TN 37148-1729

Or call our toll-free number:
1-800-286-7166

You can also request a catalog online. Visit us at our Website!
www.justpretend.com

Ask for Stardust Classics at your library or bookstore.